LONDON CALLING!

MYDWORTH MYSTERIES #3

Neil Richards • Matthew Costello

RED DOG

UK

LONDON CALLING!

PROLOGUE

Lizzie Spence lay on her bed, listening to the night-time sounds of the house, watching through her heavy lace curtains for the first hint of sunrise, barely able to believe what she was about to do.

I'm running away from home, she thought. *Me! Timid little Lizzie. Lizzie in the corner, Lizzie head down, Lizzie never say "boo" to a goose! Nobody will* ever *believe it!*

Running away from boring, dull, nothing-ever-happens Mydworth.

Running away to London!

Running away to seek fame and fortune!

For what felt like the hundredth time, she checked the little clock on her bedside table. Twenty to five in the morning. Just five more minutes, then up she'd get. Bag packed – hidden underneath the bed and ready to go.

Then, out of the house in the near darkness, down to Mydworth station and onto the milk train to London. Her adventure beginning. Her first steps to the West End, stardom, then – who knows? – maybe Broadway, or even Hollywood and the talkies!

Just like her screen idols, Clara Bow, Greta Garbo, Mary Pickford, Betty Balfour.

Wasn't this *exactly* how they started? Chasing a dream, defying their stuffy old parents, running away to the theatre?

Oh! She absolutely couldn't wait to meet them, or imagine – working with them, laughing with them – sharing this story with them!

How she too escaped!

She knew – *without a doubt* – that would happen.

She checked her clock again. Saw beside it the little note she'd left Mum. Felt a pang of guilt, but pushed it away.

Quarter to five.

Yes. *Time to go.*

Barely able to contain her excitement, she slipped off the bed (already dressed, coat on) grabbed her bag, and then picked up Teddy, popped him in her pocket. Sure, she was a big girl, but still, mustn't forget Teddy.

She crept to the door and opened it as gently as she could, afraid of the creaky floorboards sending up an alarm.

She looked across the landing in the darkness. Her parents' room – door shut. From within, the reassuring sound of both of them snoring.

Upstairs in the attic room, she knew Ellen the maid would be sleeping soundly too. *(God – who wouldn't be, the hours Ellen worked?)*

Heart pounding, she closed the bedroom door behind her, tiptoed along the landing, then down the stairs, concentrating so hard, not letting her little leather case bang on the banisters.

At the front door, she heard the old grandfather clock chime the third quarter – silly old clock, always slow, always had been.

Silly, she thought, *yes, but also, beautiful. Would it be one of the things from this big old house she would miss?*

For a second, she felt a pang of real fear at this amazing, dangerous step she was taking, and looked around the hallway as the first soft glow of dawn began to filter through the little stained-glass windows by the front door.

LONDON CALLING!

Then she shook the fear away. No! There could be no turning back. She had to get out of here. Seize the future! It's 1929, and the world is changing!

Wasn't that what Oliver had said to her at the dance academy?

"Make your own life, kid," he'd said, his eyes all twinkly. *"You're one in a million. I can tell. You're special and you, young lady, are going to be a star."*

After that, Lizzie knew she would never forgive herself if she stayed here in stuffy Mydworth, got married to some boring, pompous man who probably worked in the City and snored all night, did the rounds of church and sherry parties and bridge evenings and the tennis club.

Her whole life – so *boring*!

God no!

She wanted – no, *needed* – the bright lights, the cheering crowds, the cameras, the red carpets!

So – she opened the front door and stepped out onto the spotless tiled steps and breathed in the summer dawn smells of Mydworth.

Maybe for the last time. Why would she ever come back?

Then she quietly closed the door behind her, and walked down the drive to the road that led to Mydworth station – and her dreams.

1.

THE WOMEN'S VOLUNTARY SERVICE

Kat Reilly – or rather "Lady Mortimer" as she was slowly (and reluctantly) getting used to being called – wiped her paint-spattered hands on her overalls, and stepped back from the office wall she'd been painting.

"Ta-da!" she said, turning to Melissa and the Women's Voluntary Service Director, Nicola Green, who stood together in the far corner of the new WVS office, unloading books from crates and filling shelves. "So – what do you two think? Pretty good paint job?"

The two women stopped their work and came over, stepping around the worm-eaten loose floorboards of the shabby, dilapidated room.

"I'd say you've missed your vocation, Kat," said Nicola.

Kat loved that Nicola had absolutely no problem dispensing with any of that "Lady" rigmarole.

"Love the colour," said Melissa.

"Shame half the can seems to have ended up in my hair," said Kat. "Does it say it'll wash out? *Do* hope so. Not sure lime green is my shade! Okay then – what's next?"

LONDON CALLING!

She watched as Nicola Green lit another of her foul-smelling cigarettes, spat out a loose bit of tobacco, and scanned the room.

Not a habit that Kat ever – what was the word they used here? – *fancied*.

Nicola – in her tweed jacket, faded blouse and ancient slacks – always looked to Kat like she should be in a vegetable patch somewhere, maybe planting potatoes. Or a cattle ranch, if Sussex had such things.

Kat watched her tug at a light switch in a section of wall that seemed to be only staying up thanks to the Victorian wallpaper.

"Don't suppose you also know anything about electrical wiring?" said Nicola, as chunks of plaster crumbled to the floor. "The other rooms were okay – but I think this lot here needs replacing."

"Now *there* you've got me. Paint's the limit of my housebuilding skills. Though I can hammer the odd nail, albeit none too accurately."

"No matter. I know a chap who could do it," said Melissa, the WVS's newest – and so far only – recruit. "Billy Pagett, over at the garage. Handy with all sorts of things!"

"We wouldn't be able to pay him," said Nicola quickly. "Well, maybe a bit." She shot a look back to Kat. "We need to watch every shilling!"

"Oh, don't worry about that," said Melissa, grinning. "He's awfully struck with me. If I ask, he'll do it for nothing, I'm sure."

"Well, okay then. That's fair enough," said Nicola.

"Isn't that worker exploitation, Nicola?" said Kat, teasing the old suffragette.

"Not at all. He gains the admiration and respect of our young Melissa here. I'd say that's a good deal!" said Nicola, laughing.

She walked over to the bay window that looked down onto Mydworth's Market Square. "Anyway, we do have to get this place up and running, I can't keep meeting people at my home. Talk about needing repairs!"

Nicola opened the window and flicked the ash from her cigarette.

Kat knew Nicola lived and breathed this work – the WVS was a lifeline for women for miles around who came with every problem under the sun, hoping for a sympathetic, confidential ear. And often desperately needing help.

And finding – sometimes with the assistance of Kat and her husband Harry – a solution to their troubles.

Yet, just a few weeks ago it had seemed that the organisation must close. No base of operations, having been told to vacate the dingy room above the dress shop. And almost no funds.

But then, an anonymous donor had stepped forward, enabling Nicola to rent this near-derelict house on the square, with its all-important rear alleyway and discreet entrance.

"Women who come to us," she'd said, *"are often under threat of violence, Kat. They're so brave reaching out for help. The least we can do is make sure they can get that help without being seen."*

The money had also been enough to fund a young assistant – Melissa Shreeve – who'd seen first-hand the work that Kat, Nicola and Harry could do and had instantly volunteered her time.

Kat had already seen how Melissa – just eighteen years old – could tap into the world of the younger folk of Mydworth in a way that she and Nicola couldn't possibly manage.

Together, the three of them had spent the last month gutting the three floors of the building – painting, decorating, dragging in furniture. This top floor was the last to be done – and now the real work could begin.

LONDON CALLING!

"Tell you what," said Nicola, turning back in to the room. "Why don't you two get yourselves washed up while I—"

But before she could finish, the telephone rang on the floor below, the sound shrill and loud in the empty building.

"—answer the phone," said Nicola, and Kat watched her head quickly downstairs.

Kat changed out of her tattered overalls. Melissa did so too. Then one after the other, they washed in the cold water of the sink in the bare bathroom.

By the time Kat saw Nicola appear again, she was dressed and ready to go home.

"Favour to ask, Kat," said Nicola.

"Sure – shoot."

"You and Harry around this evening?"

"Um, should be," said Kat. "Harry's due back from London on the five-thirty train."

"Excellent!" said Nicola. "That phone call? Need you – both of you – to drop in on someone in the town. Talk to them, if you could."

"Sounds urgent," said Kat.

"I think it might be. I'll give you the details."

"What's the problem?"

"Missing person," said Nicola.

"Really? We deal with those?" said Kat. "I thought that was generally a job for the police."

"Right. In this instance though, the police don't seem to agree that the person is actually 'missing'."

"Ah," said Kat, guessing what the story might be. "Somebody's husband? They *usually* come back, don't they?"

"No, not that," said Nicola, looking at Melissa then back to Kat. "It's a young woman."

"Oh. I see," said Kat.

Nicola turned to Melissa. "Why don't you head home, my dear, while I talk this through with Kat? And thank you so, so much for your hard work today."

"Glad to help, really am," said Melissa. "See you both on Monday?"

"You bet. Have a great weekend, kid," said Kat, smiling.

Kat waited while Melissa grabbed her coat and bag and headed home.

Then Nicola, who clearly didn't want Melissa in on this – at least not yet – told Kat about the disturbing disappearance of Lizzie Spence.

2.

CONCERNED PARENTS

Sir Harry Mortimer stepped off the five-thirty train from Victoria, tucked his copy of *The Times* under his arm, and briskly headed up Station Road towards Mydworth with the other London commuters.

Those commuters – more like a well-ordered herd, Harry thought.

And, as for Harry, he wasn't exactly sure this was quite how he'd pictured his work with the Foreign Office.

It was beginning to feel, well, all rather domestic and tame!

The stroll was becoming a familiar one since he'd returned to the little Sussex town a few months back with his new wife Kat, after years abroad in government service.

He nodded and smiled at his fellow workers as, one by one, they scurried off home in different directions, no doubt looking forward to a weekend away from the bustle and noise and smoke of the city.

Office workers, clerks, bankers, a smattering of civil servants, all – like him – in their workaday suits and hats. He smiled to himself. None of them would have guessed his own rather unusual role in a discreet government department in St James's Park.

Discreet – and also most secret.

Even Kat wasn't really allowed to know the details. Not that he kept much from her. He'd trust her with his life.

She certainly knew the work was a continuation of his Cairo posting and was subject to the Official Secrets Act.

Having herself worked for some years in a similar role for the US State Department, she knew not to ask too many questions, and Harry appreciated this.

It was still light – *the wonder of summer!* – as he crossed Market Square and headed up the little cobbled street towards the old church and their house that was tucked behind it.

The Dower House, several months on, was still not quite decorated, though they had made a well-stocked cocktail cart – silver shakers and an array of spirits – a priority.

He passed through their gate, and as he walked up the gravel drive he loosened his tie and took off his hat – *so* looking forward to a little domestic time with his beautiful American wife. That oh-so-welcome gin and tonic together as they strolled in the garden planning shrubs and beds, or sat chatting about the day's events before dinner.

Though he sometimes worried that this life here in Sussex might not prove exciting enough for her. He knew his Kat, and the girl from the Bronx liked her *excitements*.

As he reached the step, he saw the front door open – Kat standing there, coat on, handbag on her shoulder.

Dressed, not in her more customary slacks, but, as if she was off to meet someone.

Curious…

"The warrior returns," she said, stepping close.

"Lady Mortimer."

"Sir Harry."

They kissed.

"Well," he said after a few seconds. "How about this evening we skip the gin and jump straight to the main course?"

LONDON CALLING!

She kissed him again, her eyes soft.

"Would love to—"

Her blue-green eyes were wide, clearly speaking the truth.

"But?"

"Exactly," she said. "*But.*"

"Ah, right," he said, stepping back now, taking on his best detective pose. "Let me guess. Coat. Bag. Smart shoes. We've been invited out?"

"Something like that," she said, reaching in and doing up his tie again, then taking his hat from his hand and perching it on his head.

"Don't tell me. A case?" said Harry.

"A case indeed."

"Time to hit the cocktails before or..."

"Might have to wait," said Kat.

Then he watched as she took his briefcase and his *Times*, placed them in the hallway, shut the door behind them, and took his arm.

"Sounds urgent," he said.

"I'll tell you all about it – or as much as I know – on the way," she said, and together they turned and walked back down the drive.

"SIX WEEKS AGO," said Kat, as they crossed the road by the church and headed down High Street, "Lizzie Spence – twenty-one years old, daughter of Aubrey and Glenys Spence, upright citizens of Mydworth both – ran away to seek her fortune in the West End of London."

"Ah, that old tale. The lure of the bright lights. Smell of the greasepaint, eh?"

"Something like that. Trouble is, Harry – apart from a couple of postcards – the parents haven't heard a word from her."

She looked straight at her husband as he pondered this.

"Glenys, the mother, is beside herself with worry and has conjured up all kinds of terrible fates that might have befallen the poor girl."

"And from what I know of the West End," Harry said, "her imagination may not be too far off the reality. What about the police?"

"Ah yes. Well, Sergeant Timms says, unfortunately, the young girl is old enough to do what she likes. She's clearly gone of her own volition and, therefore, they can't help."

"Sounds about right to me. Hands tied, and so on," said Harry. "Twenty-one? I mean, she *is* an adult after all."

"You're all heart, Harry."

"Now hang on. I feel for them. The girl too. Still, the law's the law."

Kat shook her head. "Well, I do hope you won't take that attitude when our daughter runs away from home."

"Ah, you see, that's where you get a bit *off course*, Kat darling. Daughter of ours? Never run away from home, because she'll simply love us too much. And besides – I thought you said we were going to have lots of sons? Thinking cricket, rugby, and—"

"Any daughter of ours will enjoy all that as well."

"With you as her mother, I don't doubt it. Now, when exactly were you planning on launching this 'sons and daughters' scheme of ours?"

Kat grinned. "We'll just have to see about that. Your family values will have to improve first."

"Got it. Being a thoroughly modern husband isn't that easy you know."

Kat reached up and touched his shoulder. *Always so good to have him by her side. And so much fun to be with.*

LONDON CALLING!

"But seriously, Kat, nobody can make a grown woman stay with Mum and Dad if she doesn't want to."

Kat stopped at the corner of Market Square. Though she knew the centre of town now, she still hadn't worked out the maze of streets that surrounded it. "Rosemary Lane — it's down here, somewhere, isn't it?"

"Straight down, second left, I seem to remember," said Harry, taking her arm now and leading the way.

"Here's the thing, Harry. I don't think they want to bring Lizzie home," continued Kat, "they just want to know where she is — and that she's safe."

"Ah well. That's reasonable enough," said Harry as he stopped at a last corner of terraced houses. "Here we are — Rosemary Lane. One of the most respectable roads in Mydworth, I'll have you know." He leaned into her. "And absolutely *filled* with respectable people. Now, what's the number we're looking for?"

Kat looked down the tree-lined road. She could see larger houses set back in wide gardens. "Not a number. Called… Elm Croft."

"Do hope they have a helpful sign outside. Otherwise this might be more challenging than it ought to be."

Together they walked slowly down the lane in the ebbing light, checking the names on the gates, the houses looking solid and, yes, respectable. Lawns neatly cropped; cars in most of the driveways.

At the end of the lane, they finally came to "Elm Croft", all mock Tudor gables and mullioned windows.

Kat took in the big garden, the large sedan parked out front.

"Well, this has to be worth a bob or two," said Harry as they walked up the drive. "Think if we take this 'case' you should ask the Spences for a very generous WVS donation."

"Oh, don't you worry," said Kat. "Nicola's made that clear already."

And she stepped up onto the porch and rang the bell.

AFTER A MINUTE, the door opened slowly. A tired looking woman in a woollen dress and cardigan, neat pearl necklace, and low heels, peered round the door at them suspiciously.

"Mrs Spence?" said Kat, smiling. "I'm from the WVS. I believe Nicola Green told you I'd be coming over?"

"*Lady* Mortimer?" said the woman, as if confused by Kat's American accent.

"And Sir Harry Mortimer," said Harry, putting out his hand to shake the woman's. She took it, limply. "At your service."

"Y-you'd better come in," she said, opening the door and ushering them in, then closing it swiftly behind them as if worried the neighbours would see.

Kat looked at Harry, who raised his eyebrows in return.

He, too, had noticed the woman's nervousness.

HARRY SAT on the pristine sofa. Kat took notes. Harry sipped his tea, watching Mrs Spence carefully as she recounted the events surrounding her daughter's departure.

He and Kat had worked together on a few cases now, and seemed instinctively to know when one should do the talking and the other the listening.

Both, so important.

"We hadn't an inkling. None at all. You see, it was a Saturday, and we all sleep a little later on a Saturday. I went into Lizzie's room around ten and that's when I saw the bed empty! And just a note on the side."

"Could we see the note, Mrs Spence?" said Kat.

Harry watched the woman open her handbag and hand it over to Kat, who read it then passed it to Harry.

"It doesn't say much, does it?" said Mrs Spence. "*'Going to London. Will let you know soon as I've got work. Theatre interviews already set up. Don't worry about me.'* See? I know it by heart. Hardly worth writing. Made Aubrey so terribly angry."

"Aubrey – that's Mr Spence?" said Harry. He saw her nod. "Would it be possible to talk to him?" he said.

"Aubrey's not home yet. From London."

Harry sensed the woman's tension talking about her husband.

"Ah," he said, "that's a shame. When are you expecting him?"

"Fridays… he's often late."

"He works in the City?"

"Imperial Fidelity," said Mrs Spence. "He's a partner."

Harry nodded. He knew of Imperial, an old and eminently respectable investment house, which looked after funds for, among others, the Church of England.

And, Harry imagined, having a daughter run away to join the theatre might not play well at the office.

"Was this the first you knew that Lizzie wanted to be an actress?" said Kat.

"Oh, she's been going on about it for years, but we never took her seriously, you know? Thought she'd grow out of it. Get a secretarial job somewhere, settle down, meet somebody *solid*. I mean, that's what's supposed to happen, isn't it?"

"And does she have any, um, connections, in the theatre world?" asked Harry.

"I hardly think so!" said Mrs Spence, as if the very idea were scandalous. "She's lived her whole life here in Mydworth! But what do I know? After this, I'm not sure I know her at all!"

"Is she an outgoing sort of girl?" said Kat. "You know, parties, lots of pals, tennis and so on?"

"No, not at all. Only thing she does – and very seriously, mind you – is her dance class."

"And where does that happen?" said Kat.

"At the Town Hall," said Mrs Spence. "There's a company comes over from Chichester, runs them every Saturday morning."

"Good Lord," said Harry. "Dance classes – right here in Mydworth!"

From the look on Kat's face, he could tell… *now not the time for humour.*

He turned back to the girl's mother.

"Perhaps there are people at the dance class who might know where she went?"

"Oh, Aubrey tried that, the Saturday after she left. Went down there. Spoke to the woman in charge. But she didn't know *anything.* Least, so she said."

"What's the name of the company?" said Kat, pencil ready at her notebook.

"The De Souza Academy of Dance and Drama."

"De Souza?" said Harry.

"Woman who runs it. Constanza de Souza. She's not *English*, of course."

"Of course," said Harry nodding sympathetically.

Clearly in Mrs Spence's eyes, being "not English" was obviously tantamount to being a potential *ne'er-do-well.*

England hadn't changed much, Harry thought, in his years abroad.

LONDON CALLING!

"Mrs Spence – was Lizzie a good dancer?" said Kat. "Talented? Do you think she could make it in London?"

"I have absolutely *no* idea," said Mrs Spence, with a shrug.

"You never saw her perform?"

"Well, yes, in a few shows they staged. And was it good? These days all they do is jump around isn't it? Is that really dancing? Indecent too! The very names make one shudder. The Shimmy. The Black Bottom. Not in my day!"

Harry looked at Kat. She was being so patient with this woman, who it was becoming quite clear didn't know much about her daughter's life.

"You did say you've had a couple of postcards from Lizzie," said Harry. "Do you have them to hand as well?"

Mrs Spence nodded, as she dipped in her handbag again and handed them over to Harry.

Both tourist snapshots of London landmarks – buses, Big Ben. And on the message side, just reassuring words and phrases "everything going well", "lots of chorus jobs", "more work than I can cope with", "will pop home when I can", "Hollywood here I come!"

He checked the postmarks. They were both London W1. No other clues as to her whereabouts. No return address or telephone number.

He passed them to Kat.

"What about a photograph of Lizzie?" said Harry. "One we could take?"

"You mean… you think… you two might help us?"

Harry looked at Kat as she answered.

"Possibly."

Mrs Spence fumbled in her handbag and brought out a dog-eared photo, handed it to Kat, who then passed it over.

"You know," Harry said. "Perhaps she is just as she says, very busy. Young people – they can easily forget to be in touch, can't they?"

But the look in Mrs Spence's eyes chilled Harry.

"Not my Lizzie," said Mrs Spence. "She's in trouble, I *know* it. Feel it in my bones."

Harry heard the front door open and saw the woman look up suddenly, a flash of alarm visible on her face.

"Oh dear," she said, leaning forward and almost whispering. "That's Aubrey now. I must warn you – he wasn't at all happy when I told him I'd asked for help—"

But before she could finish, the door to the sitting room opened and Harry saw, framed in the entrance, a man he guessed was Aubrey Spence: City coat and hat still on, face pink, eyes dark behind small round spectacles.

"Glenys!" he said, his voice *dripping* – Harry thought – with equal amounts of alarm and suspicion. "What the *devil* is going on? I thought I told you we didn't need help?"

Harry stood up instinctively and offered his hand. "Mr Spence... Sir Harry Mortimer—"

"I know who you are, Sir Harry. And your wife, Lady Mortimer." A bit of a nod towards Kat. "I can *assure* you both, this is nothing personal. What has happened to our daughter is a private family matter. *We* shall deal with it."

Kat also stood. "Mr Spence, I completely understand. But, you see, your wife asked us here to help, and I believe we can. Sir Harry and I, well, we have a bit of experience with such things. So, if you'll just let us—"

"Mrs Spence is mistaken. And now I simply must ask you to leave. My apologies for any inconvenience. I trust you will forget the whole matter." Then he added, his voice direct, "And say nothing to anyone about it."

Harry stared at the man, Spence's anger clearly barely restrained. And, though he suspected Kat wanted to argue the case, he sensed – better to withdraw and regroup.

That military training still coming in handy.

"Quite understand, old chap," Harry said, reaching for his coat that lay on the sofa beside him. "Crossed wires, I'm sure." Then he turned to Kat. "Best we head home, leave it at that, I think."

He saw Kat open her mouth, ready to argue – then, as he gave her the slightest of winks, a signal he hoped – she, too, picked up her coat and nodded.

"Of course," she said, then turning to Mrs Spence and shaking her hand. "Thank you so much for the tea. And I do hope you have some positive news of your daughter very soon."

"Goodbye, Sir Harry," said Spence, holding out his hand. "Lady Mortimer."

But Kat didn't shake it. Harry sensed she wanted to open fire on the father with both barrels.

The bullying – definitely not Kat's cup of tea.

And he gently placed a persuasive hand on her shoulder.

"We'll see ourselves out, don't you worry," he said quickly.

Harry nudged Kat forward. As a grim Mr Spence stood to one side, they went out into the hall, opened the front door and left, without looking back.

"You know," Kat said as they reached the end of the drive, "I was ready to take his hand and instead of *shaking* it, give it—"

"Oh, I *guessed that*," Harry said laughing. "Okay then, so, Saturday tomorrow. Dance class first thing?"

"Madame de Souza? You bet," said Kat.

Harry knew that, though she was still fuming, she'd be relieved to hear his suggestion.

They were definitely on this case, if it was one.

"Then straight up to London. Find the girl – yes?"

"Absolutely," said Kat. "To hell with Mr Spence's orders to stand down."

"Curious that, don't you think? Just a matter of privacy? Family honour? I'm not so sure."

"That bull-headed man," she said a minute later, as they walked at some pace back down Rosemary Lane. "That bloody man, he–"

"Deserves a punch in the face, does he?" said Harry.

She laughed. "Too right! Followed by a swift kick in the—"

"Ahem… changing topics… brandy and sodas when we get home, don't you think?" said Harry, turning to her and pausing for a second. "Oh, and there was a rumour of a dinner on offer?"

He leaned towards her. "Or do I have that wrong, Lady Mortimer?"

She stared at him – then laughed.

"Yes – if you play your cards right," she said. "Large brandies first though. And whatever else my Sir Harry might like…"

"Oh, you Americans. You *do* know how turn a phrase."

Harry put his arm through hers and pulled her closer as they carried on walking back through the dark streets of Mydworth.

It might take more than a couple of drinks to bring his wife – his wonderful, passionate, righteous wife – back to earth after this encounter.

But she was always worth the effort.

LONDON CALLING!

3.

A CHANCE MEETING

Kat and Harry made their way through the bustling stalls of Market Square towards the Town Hall, past early morning shoppers, delivery trucks and hand carts.

Kat had been down here to shop most Saturday mornings since she'd come to Mydworth, but she'd never been inside the Town Hall that dominated the square.

She turned to Harry. "That feeling – you know? When a case starts..."

"Good, isn't it?" he said.

She pushed open the double glass doors of the imposing stone building, Harry right behind her as she went in.

To one side, she could see a hall filled with tables and shoppers – a handicraft market, it seemed.

Ahead of them, a wide flight of stairs. And as she took in the smells and sounds of the old building, she heard music from upstairs. A piano being played, and the sound of feet.

"Sounds familiar," she said.

"What? You used to dance? Thought you were busy riding all the time. What was that park near you, with stables? Van... van...?" said Harry, still discovering new facts about his wife.

"Van Cortland Park. And yes, not only did I dance, Harry – I was pretty damn good at it," said Kat, leading the way up the stairs. "Couldn't you tell from all those parties?"

"Thought that shaking a leg thing was simply natural ability. Fetching too, I might add."

"Hard work, all that. If the war hadn't happened – dance was one of my ways out of the Bronx."

"Well waddya know," said Harry in his best American accent. "True confessions – I married a hoofer."

"Hoofer? My plan – star of the show, I'll have you know."

At the top of the stairs they stopped. Ahead, through more glass double doors, Kat could see a theatre space; seats all stacked to one side, the stage curtained. On a sprung floor, lines of girls of all ages in slips and plimsolls were being drilled by a tall, angular woman in a red sheath skirt.

"Good Lord," said Harry, voice low. "Wonder how long this has been going on? In Mydworth no less!"

Kat pushed open the doors, Harry right behind her – but as she did, the woman turned and saw them.

"Carry on girls!" she called. "Chins up! Smile! Breathe! Stand tall!"

Then she hurried over, all dark hair, flashing eyes, and jewellery.

"Come in! Come *in*! Take a seat, please! Mothers always welcome!"

Kat stepped forward, then saw the woman step front of Harry, one hand gently resting on his chest, the air now drifting with heavy perfume.

"But *no* fathers, I'm afraid," she said, in Kat's opinion, rather coyly. "Ladies only, I *must* insist. Perhaps father can divert himself with a stroll around the lovely market until the class is over?"

LONDON CALLING!

Kat smiled sweetly at Harry. "I'm sure my husband completely understands. Don't you, darling?"

"But of course," said Harry. "I can be very good at diverting myself. See you downstairs, *darling*."

Kat watched him bow slightly then retreat through the double doors. She turned back to the woman.

"Welcome to the De Souza Travelling Academy of Dance and the Dramatic Arts!"

HARRY sauntered down the marble steps of the Town Hall, then leaned against one of the pillars in the reception area, wondering what to actually do while Kat checked out the dance academy.

"Talented young things, aren't they?" came a man's voice from behind him.

He turned, to see a short, wiry man – late twenties perhaps – with a waxed moustache, in a pinstripe suit and sharp shoes.

"Beg your pardon?" said Harry.

The man came closer.

"Upstairs," he said. "The young dancers. All that… enthusiasm too."

"Ah yes," said Harry. "Very talented."

"She kick you out, did she?" said the man, nodding to the rooms above.

"She did," said Harry. "My wife was given leave to remain, but I…"

"Constanza doesn't hold with any chaps hanging around. Can't say I blame her. Men, you know? Makes sense."

"Constanza?"

"De Souza. Lady what runs the academy."

"Ah. You know her?"

"Do I," said the man. He handed Harry a business card which Harry took and read: *Oliver Pleasance. Talent Scout. Affiliated to The Grosvenor Talent Agency, London W1.*

"Nice to meet you, Oliver." Harry did a quick edit to his next words. "Harry Mortimer."

"Pleased to meet you too, Harry. Smoke?"

Harry saw him slip a silver cigarette case from his jacket pocket and proffer it. "No thanks, I don't indulge."

He waited while the man flicked a petrol lighter and lit the cigarette.

"What's the game then?" said Pleasance. "Got a young 'un of your own that you want to get rid of on a Saturday morning, eh? Maybe… give you and the wife a bit of a lie in?"

Harry stared for a second, then – since the response appeared to be expected – he laughed.

Little humouring of the oily character here might go a long way, he thought.

"Ha, not exactly. But I suppose that's how it works for some is it?"

"Tell me about it! Gets the kids out the house for a couple of hours, you see. Keeps a marriage sweet, that does. Or survivable, at least. Not that I'd know. No trouble and strife for me!"

"Lucky chap!" said Harry, keeping up the "boys together" act. "What brings you down here though?"

"Part of the circuit, Harry."

"Circuit?"

"There's dance academies all over the country these days. Kids go to the talkies, see them glamour girls up on the silver screen, can't stop 'em signing up for lessons. All got stars in their eyes."

"Ah, I see. They think they can make it big, eh?"

LONDON CALLING!

"Too right," said Pleasance. Then a look of caution – and he said, "And for some, well, you never know."

"Really?"

"Oh, yes, I've seen it happen. If they got real talent – and they're hard workers – 'sky's the limit', I always say."

He took a puff of his cigarette.

"Tricky for a girl here though, surely? Mydworth's hardly New York!"

"True. But, see, that's where I come in, Harry old boy. I spot the ones with the *nous* – I get 'em up to town, see an agent. He puts 'em in a show, like a try-out, and if they do well, everybody's happy and the world goes round."

"And you get a commission?"

"Spot on. Finder's fee. Chap's gotta earn a decent crust."

"Of course," said Harry, smiling at the man. "You ever have any luck round here?"

"Now and then. Sent one or two girls on the 'path to glory' as I call it."

"How amazing. From Mydworth!"

"Who knows? Might see 'em up there with Fred Astaire one day!"

"I'll look out for them!"

Pleasance looked at Harry as if trying to gauge whether he was serious.

"So, like I said, what's your game then?" said Pleasance. "If you haven't got a daughter who wants to learn the Charleston?"

"Me?" said Harry, thinking fast. "Oh, well, my wife, she's actually looking for dance lessons. For me too, I fear. Says I'm a bit of a fuddy-duddy on the dance floor."

"Ha, well good luck, mate. These new crazes… gotta be fitter than a butcher's dog the way they jump around!"

Harry laughed and whacked him on the shoulder, playing his role. "Exactly my fear!"

Then he heard footsteps coming down the stairs.

"Ah, I fancy that's her," he said. "Better scoot."

"Me too," said Pleasance. "Grab myself a nice pork pie off one of them stalls for my breakfast."

"Good chatting to you, Oliver. Maybe see you again soon?"

"Righto, old chap. Look forward to it, Harry," said Pleasance.

In fact, I'm pretty certain I will, thought Harry as he watched the man head out through the doors into the square.

He turned as Kat reached the bottom of the stairs.

"Any luck?" he said.

"Nothing really," said Kat, shrugging. "Constanza claims to know nothing at all about Lizzie's trip to London. But, listening to her, I'm thinking she's not telling the whole truth."

"You know, that might make sense. I've just had a very interesting little talk down here. A talent scout. Supposedly. How about I tell you all about it on the way?"

"Can't wait," said Kat.

And together they walked out of the Town Hall, down the steps into Market Square.

Halfway across the square, as they threaded their way through the busy stalls, Harry felt Kat's hand on his arm.

"Don't look round for a second Harry," she said.

"What is it?" He knew she'd spotted something important.

She moved to one of the stalls selling jars of honey and jam, feigning an interest.

He moved closer to her.

"What is it?" he said.

"Over by that hardware store, in the doorway," she said, holding up a jar as if for him to inspect.

LONDON CALLING!

He casually took the jar, read its label, smiled, put it back on the counter, then glanced across at the old ironmonger's shop, thirty yards away.

There, in the shadow of the canopy over the windows, stood a man, hat pulled down over his face, watching them.

Aubrey Spence.

"I thought I saw him earlier," said Kat. "But I wasn't sure."

"It's him all right," said Harry. "Curious."

"Very," said Kat.

She took his arm and they headed back to the Dower House and their car, all packed and ready for London.

4.

PIED-À-TERRE

Kat looked out the window as the narrow roads of the countryside gave way to larger roads, and finally the streets of London.

"On your left – Waterloo Station," said Harry, as they emerged from one of his shortcuts onto a wide street lined by tall railway arches and soot-blackened buildings.

"Wow! I thought Manhattan was busy."

Kat held tight as Harry threaded the Alvis through the traffic. Cars and noisy motorbikes edged past trucks making deliveries. Red trams and buses crammed tight with passengers, shared the road with boys pushing handcarts, and men in horse-drawn carriages with full crates of leafy produce in the back.

On the pavements, a jostling crowd of Saturday workers and shoppers spilled onto the streets. And on every surface – the sides of buses, buildings and trams – were placards, adverts and posters.

"I know," Harry said, as he accelerated onto Waterloo Bridge, "that you've spent time in Paris, Istanbul and even a stint in Berlin, but this city is going to be pretty special."

"Already is," she said, not knowing which way to look as they crossed the Thames. To one side, in the distance, she could see St Paul's Cathedral, with its marble-white dome.

"Houses of Parliament, t'other way," said Harry, nodding to her left.

"And your office?"

"'Fraid you won't see it from here. Tucked round the back of the War Office, behind those big buildings there."

Kat's eye was drawn to the river, bustling with traffic: motor boats, barges, cargo boats, ships docking, cranes at work.

"And just there," said Harry, pointing as they headed towards the Strand, "most important... the Savoy Hotel. Oh, you'll love the bar."

"Can't wait," said Kat, overwhelmed by all these famous landmarks.

"Drury Lane," said Harry as they came off the bridge and the street narrowed.

"I've heard of it," said Kat. "Didn't know it was real."

"Oh, it's real all right," said Harry, flicking the car through a quick left and a right to avoid traffic jams.

With the window open, Kat heard music, a violin, the tune cutting the noise and bustle of the crowded streets.

"Look there," she said. "That musician."

"He's just trying to pick up a few *bob* from passers-by. See a lot of that these days. Ah – nearly there."

Harry turned the steering wheel of their sporty Alvis and went down the tightest of streets, before taking another sharp turn.

Kat saw a mammoth building straight ahead.

"And what is *that*?"

"Oh, that old thing? Just the British Museum. All the world's treasures, you know. The loot of an empire. We must put a visit there into our diary. I mean," he turned to her, "even in the Cairo Museum, I doubt that they have as many mummies as that place does."

He turned back.

"And I thought our Museum of Natural History was big," she said.

"Ah, here we are," said Harry. "One more turn. Have you at our little flat in a jiffy."

Our little flat, Kat thought. Their getaway apartment in London.

Now *that* was something.

"You're going to love it," Harry said, favouring her with a smile as they passed through a great square with wooded gardens in its centre. "Welcome to Bloomsbury."

This whole city, with its lettered and numbered sections – so orderly – and the quaint names that she knew of only from books: Mayfair, Soho, Notting Hill, Shepherd's Bush.

Love it?

She already did.

HARRY pulled up beside a long terrace of tall, perfectly matched red-brick apartment blocks. The stone trims of the windows and doors were painted a brilliant white; and the steps leading up to those doors were accompanied by a long-spiked metal railing.

"Our flat is *here?*"

"Yes. Nothing too flashy, of course. Six floors – we're on the first. What you Americans call the second floor of course. But it *does* have a lift."

"Think we'll manage the climb without that. Did I ever tell you about that apartment I had in the Lower East Side? Just a sub-let for a few—"

"Sub what? Oh – imagine you mean a *short* let?"

She laughed. Funny this game they had of using terms that the other didn't have a clue about.

LONDON CALLING!

All kind of fun.

"Right. I was just, you know, renting for a few months. Five-storey walkup, it was called.'

"Ah, that's where you got so fit."

"Hated those stairs. But loved the apartment."

Harry killed the ignition, and climbed out.

"Time for Lady Mortimer to inspect the premises. We'll come back for the bags."

Kat opened her door, and stepped onto the pavement. Down the street, a woman was using some kind of brambly broom to sweep the sidewalk.

Sweeping it like it's a carpet, Kat thought.

And she followed Harry up the spotless tiled steps as he got out a key to open the front door.

HARRY pulled the grating of the tiny lift closed and fastened it shut.

"You know," Kat said, "we could have just walked up."

"And miss all the excitement in here? The ride up? Besides, you need to know how to operate this contraption. See, won't work unless this gate is latched, then you just hit the button like this and—"

"Harry, if you remember... I have lived in buildings with elevators."

"Yes, right. Well, *voila.* Up we go."

The lift shook and Harry felt Kat tumble into him.

This city, the flat, the time we'll spend here... So looking forward to showing her, thought Harry.

Hopefully to be as much a part of their life as Mydworth.

He looked at her. Inches away. *Perfect time for a kiss,* he thought.

As the lift reached the first floor, someone stood waiting: a woman in a grey hat that looked like a stack of pancakes, topped with a faux faded rose; her face looking as rumpled as her hat. A matching grey skirt and jacket, and formidable shoes – ladies' brogues – completed the look.

Her eyes glowered as if her wait for the lift had been caused by them.

So, all in all, maybe a good thing he hadn't stolen that kiss.

One can risk only so much opprobrium.

With the lady looking on, he undid the gate and they stepped out, squeezing past the bulldog of a woman.

"Good afternoon, madam," he said to her, full-on charm.

"Hmmph," she said, stepping into the lift and sliding the metal grates shut.

"We're this way," he said to Kat, both of them trying not to giggle, as the woman gave them one last withering look before she disappeared *en route* to the ground floor, and Harry took Kat to the door of their London pied-à-terre.

KAT WALKED into the apartment, expecting a tight corridor, a tiny sitting room, and a small kitchen and bedroom nearby.

But this was something else.

The entry foyer was open – spacious – with a vase of flowers on a small table by the door. The wide corridor ahead led to a sitting room facing the street below.

She walked directly to that room and took it in: its curve of nearly ceiling-high windows, sheer curtains letting in light while preserving privacy, hardwood floor, Turkish rugs, sleek furniture. At one end, a fireplace and sofas – at the other, a dining table.

Modern art on the walls. Abstracts. In a corner, a small cocktail bar and a gramophone-radio.

She turned to Harry.

"It's beautiful."

"Think it will do at a pinch?"

"I'll say."

Then she walked into a small kitchen. Not a place to prepare a meal for a lot of guests, but certainly serviceable for the two of them.

"Oh," Harry said, standing by the windows, backlit by the afternoon sun. "Actually, it has a bedroom, too, you know."

Striding past Harry, noting his cheeky grin, she entered the bedroom, the bed topped with a shiny, Asian-themed purple coverlet. An Art Deco dressing table and mirror stood to one side, and the *en suite* WC to the other.

"Harry. This place…"

"Pass muster?"

"I love it. But I have a few questions."

"I'm all answers."

"You had this furnished all by yourself?"

"Suppose I did, really. Put it together over the years. Bit of help from a local decorator to freshen up the place a few months back. And, yes, while I was still away, Maggie popped up to town, checked things over for me."

Kat wasn't surprised that Harry's housekeeper took an interest in the place.

"And the flowers?"

"Oh, these buildings, the flats, all have a handy 'madame' to attend to regular cleaning, accepting packages, tending to things like the need for roses and daffodils. Just have to ring ahead."

Then Kat had another thought.

A very different kind of question.

"Harry, you've had this pied-à-terre a long time?"

"Been in the family for years. Aunt Lavinia used to live here, and then, you know, when my parents died she moved down to Mydworth Manor, to look after me. Then, after the war, she was pretty settled down in Sussex so I took over the lease. Handy for the office, you know?"

"Not what I meant," she said.

And at that, she saw a cautious look cross Harry's face.

"Okay, what then, Lady Mortimer?"

"You having this flat – I mean when you were younger. While you were working at the Foreign Office. Ever use it for—"

"Ah, said the fox. You mean, did I ever, in my wild London days, lure someone up here, perhaps for a spot of brandy…?"

"And *whatever*?"

Harry crossed the room.

"Well, excellent question, my dear. *Very* sharp. I can report, with total confidence, that I have only brought one female up here with any thought of a brandy and – who knows." He paused, raising a hand to her cheek. "And that person, is you."

Tour over, things to be done, it was Kat who leaned close and kissed her ever-surprising husband.

HARRY SAT down at the dining-room table, with its leaves now folded down – a perfect table for two.

"Time to plan what we're going to do to find this Lizzie Spence."

"Had an idea about that," said Kat.

"Yes, I thought you would."

"We have the photo. Your West End isn't far from here?"

LONDON CALLING!

"A brisk walk, but, yes, Leicester Square, Piccadilly... all relatively close."

"We go to the theatres, ask around. Show the photo."

"Lot of people to ask. Lot of theatres."

"Worth trying, no?"

"Absolutely. We can grab a bite to eat on the way at the Lyons Corner House on Shaftesbury Avenue."

"Corner House? Sounds very exotic."

"Oh, believe me it *is*. An English institution. Five floors of goodies. Meanwhile, I'll ring up Alfie – you remember, my old batman from my flying days? Get him to meet us this evening. There's a grand pub in that area, near St Martin's. The Lamb and Flag."

"Think he can help?"

"Here's the thing about Alfie. You see, he's been on both sides of the constabulary. *Knows* people. And he knows people who know people. Be good to see if he can ask around." Harry nodded. "London, as you may get to see, has a bit of underbelly here and there."

"Surely not here in Bloomsbury?"

"Well, we are far from the days of old Jack the Ripper and the shady ladies of the Ten Bells Pub. But not *too* far."

"Interesting."

"But first, I want to call this Grosvenor Talent Agency," he said, taking out the card that Pleasance had given him.

"What are you thinking?"

"Talent agency, worked with Pleasance, and therefore probably the esteemed Madame de Souza too. Let's see what Mr Grosvenor recalls."

Harry shot a glance to a side table by the love seat that faced the fireplace – on it, a very modern-looking telephone.

"With a bit of luck, that new-fangled device is up and running."

He strode over, picked it up and listened for a dial tone.

"No need to go through the operator – apparently," he said. "Just dial the number yourself."

"Amazing," said Kat. "What will they think of next?"

"Indeed," said Harry. "Think we'll have to wait a few years before Mydworth has one of these!"

And he started dialling.

LONDON CALLING!

5.

WALKING THE WEST END

Kat looked at Harry, as he finished dialling the number from the card in his other hand.

His face showing – so far – no one was answering.

Then, his eyes widened.

"Is this the Grosvenor Talent Agency? Good. *Excellent.* Like to speak with Cedric Grosvenor. Um, no, he wouldn't necessarily know me. But I think, well, it's something that pertains to his business."

Harry grinned at her as he lied to the receptionist at the other end.

"Splendid."

He lowered the receiver and covered the mouthpiece.

"Amazing what a bit of persistence can do."

THE RECEIVER back to his ear, Harry looked out of the nearby windows.

"Why yes, Mr Grosvenor? Sir Harry Mortimer here. Yes, um, I was given your card by a mutual acquaintance."

"Yes, Sir Harry, how can be of assistance?

"You see, well my wife – Lady Mortimer – and I are looking into the matter of a young woman who has vanished."

Harry let the statement hang a bit. Hard to gauge Cedric Grosvenor's reaction to the question without seeing his expression.

"Vanished? Dear me, how distressing."

"Exactly. The girl's mother? So *very* upset. Distraught, one might say."

Kat had walked beside him. Leaned close, so – he guessed – she could pick up some of Grosvenor's response.

"I can imagine. But – um, Sir Harry – how can we at the Grosvenor Agency help you in this matter?"

Harry saw Kat nod. A slight tilt of the head, signalling – *go on. Press the man hard.*

"Now, the young lady in question came up to the Big City a few weeks back, seeking fame and fortune. Dancer, you see."

"Ah, a familiar story, Sir Harry."

"Oh really?"

"It is a sad fact of life, sir, that as theatrical agents we are often importuned by such hopeful, yet naïve, young women."

"I can only imagine. And when that happens…?"

"We inform their parents – and there the matter ends." Grosvenor cleared his throat. "Usually."

"I'm sure the parents appreciate it."

"Invariably, they do. Tell you what, Sir Harry. If you can furnish me with a name, I would be happy to pass it around among my acquaintances in the theatrical world? Make some discreet enquiries for you?"

"Oh, very kind of you, Mr Grosvenor. Her name… Lizzie Spence."

"Lizzie Spence," said Grosvenor slowly, as if writing it down.

"Doesn't ring a bell?" said Harry.

"No, I'm afraid not. Is there a special reason why it should?"

"Apparently Lizzie studied dance with a 'Constanza de Souza', who appears to be an associate of one of your employees, one Oliver Pleasance."

A gamble, that statement, Harry knew.

"Ah. Mr Pleasance. *Not* actually an employee, I must make that very clear."

"But you know him?"

"To my cost," said Grosvenor. "Chap's a bit of a 'stringer', you know. Always has some kind of little scam under way. Let me guess – he gave you the impression he can get girls work in the West End, eh?"

"That he did."

A long pause.

"And mentioned my name?"

"Correct again."

"Dammit. Stuff and nonsense, I'm afraid. Doesn't work like that – and I shall take Pleasance to task for *that* liberty if he ever dares show his face in my office."

"Ah, I see. Well. Perhaps, as you say, you could pass the name around. *Lizzie Spence.*"

"Absolutely. Dreadful situation, I'm sure."

Again, Harry paused. Grosvenor sounded genuine.

Then he looked at Kat's eyes. If suspicion could change eye colour, it was doing exactly that right now.

"Is that all, Sir Harry?" said Grosvenor. "I have clients I must attend to. I'm sorry. Good luck with your endeavours."

"Thank you for your time, Mr Grosvenor."

Harry shot a grin at Kat.

"If we have any questions, you can be sure I'll ring you back."

To which Grosvenor gave a simple, "Absolutely. Any time. Pleasure talking to you."

Harry put the receiver down and shrugged.

"Dead end," he said. Then he saw the suspicion still in her eyes. "You don't think?"

"He sounded very helpful, that's for sure. But isn't it funny that he didn't feel the need to ask for any information about Lizzie. Age? Looks? Dancer? Actress?"

"God – you're right. As if he knew the answers already?"

"Just a theory."

"I *always* like your theories," said Harry.

"Also, tell you another thing, I have never, *ever*, met a guy I liked with the name 'Cedric'."

"Really?" said Harry, smiling. "Well that seals it then, doesn't it? Let's give it a day, see what the word is on the street about Cedric Grosvenor, and then maybe go pay him a visit."

"Face to face. Yes, great," said Kat. "Now – lunch?"

"Spot on!"

FOUR HOURS later, just off Drury Lane, down a narrow alleyway, Kat stood close to the stage door of the Gaiety Theatre.

She saw Harry check his watch.

"We're due to meet Alfie in a bit."

"Last one on the list, Harry."

"Good. This going from theatre to theatre… hasn't been a roaring success, has it?"

She and Harry had been speaking to whomever they could roust in the theatres to come and speak with them, just hours away from evening performances.

"Batting zero," she told Harry. An expression, the derivation of which she had to explain. "Baseball," she had said. "And the batter keeps missing."

At that, the stage door popped open as if wedged too tight in its frame. Kat almost didn't see the man who had just effected the opening: short, squat, a chuck of cigar wedged in his mouth, and cloth cap on his head.

"What *yers* want? The girl at the ticket office… she says it was important. Tell you two what's 'urgent'… getting that bloody show running inside this outdated barn!"

The Gaiety, Kat had noted from the marquee outside, was featuring a show dubbed the "London Follies".

The star names in bold meant nothing to Kat, but below the title performers, the "Follies" promised "Dancing! Singing! Romance and Adventure!"

No sparing of the exclamation marks there.

"Are you the stage manager?" she said to the squat man.

He rolled his bulbous head at that question as if either it was obvious or totally wrong.

Take your pick.

"This show… this outfit? Big hit – but you know what? Everyone still does a bit of everything."

Having had similar conversations as they traipsed around the West End, Kat wasted no time.

"We're looking for a girl. She came to London, looking for work – to perform – and has gone missing."

At that, with the photo extended in his direction, the stage manager took off his cap, rubbed his hand through the few wisps of hair that still remained and, as if necessary, for what was to follow, removed the cigar stub from his mouth.

But before speaking, he did lean close, and stare at the picture.

42

"Pretty one. Got nice eyes. But then——" he looked up to Kat, and then Harry, "don't they all."

Harry cleared his throat. "But the point is Mr…"

"Coyne."

"Mr Coyne, have you seen her? Auditioning, or——"

Now the hat went back on his head, a signal perhaps. *Dialogue over.* The cigar, still thankfully unlit, also popped back in.

"No. And I tell you what. You seem like a nice couple. Maybe take in a show *yerselves* from time to time, eh? Even if I *did* see her, right? What are the odds I'd remember? So many girls, come here, like… er… what are *them* insects?"

"Moths?" Kat guessed.

"Yeah. Them things. They go right to the flame, don't they? And some of them…"

He left the rest of the sentence unfinished.

"Another look," Kat suggested.

And though Stage Manager Coyne probably wanted to get back to the pre-show mayhem inside the theatre, he took a moment, looking Kat right in the eye. "Yer worried, eh? I'll tell you this: from what I know – the things that happen – well, you got good reason to be."

And, at that, he leaned close and took one more look, the slow shake of his head not without a hint of remorse. "Good luck. Here," a look around the alleyway signifying the great city they were in, "you're going to need it."

And at that, the great metal stage door slammed shut behind the man.

LONDON CALLING!

6.

A PINT WITH ALFIE

Kat and Harry walked slowly away from the Strand; that wide street easily rivalling the bustle, if not the expanse, of Broadway. Though for Kat, walking around here was all rather disorienting. Compared to the orderly grid that was Midtown Manhattan, these streets of London seemed purposely designed to resemble a maze.

"All this," she said, feeling a bit defeated, "going to the theatres? Seems kinda pointless."

Harry didn't answer right away, just took her hand and they walked.

She looked down at the cobblestones below them. At one point they had to dodge a place where someone's horse had relieved itself, the results left to sit there until the rain – or street cleaners maybe – would swipe it away.

Now crossing Bow Street, she saw cars and pedestrians going back and forth, the flow looking confused and random. Some heading to pubs, she guessed, some home. Some ready for a show, dinner.

"Tell you what, Kat. After we have our chat with Alfie, how about" – his hand linked to hers – "we head over to the Berkeley?"

"Berkeley?"

"Hotel on Piccadilly. Smashing place for a cocktail and – if we can get a table – quite a passable dinner. Discuss what exactly we're doing here."

"If anything."

Harry nodded at that.

"Sorry, Harry. Feeling a tad overwhelmed. First day in London, wandering around, asking questions."

"And getting nowhere?"

"That's what it feels like," she said. "Meanwhile – somewhere out there, on one of these streets, is Lizzie Spence. Alone maybe. In trouble? Lost?"

Harry stopped, put his hands gently on her shoulders, and for a few seconds the hubbub and the jostling crowds seemed to disappear.

"We'll find her, Kat. We will."

She looked at his face and felt her own confidence lift again. She smiled.

"You're right," she said. "We will."

He took her hand again, and they headed off.

As they crossed another busy street, she and Harry joined the throng bristling left and right. Men in sharp suits and perfectly creased hats. Workers shuffling by with boxes of tools. Drivers trying out the horns on their new cars, as if a steady stream of gooselike honks would make the traffic go faster.

As they walked.

"Traffic wasn't like this when I was here last," he said.

"There will come a day when all these streets have stop lights."

"Well, by then – pied-à-terre or no pied-à-terre – I hope for us to be in the sunny hills of Provence, maybe growing our own grapes."

"Making our own wine?"

"Who knows? Anything's possible. And with you beside me to help…"

And Kat laughed. When she was feeling a little low – like now, with their zero results – he had such a great knack of helping her just *shake it off.*

She had to remember to do the same for him when the time came.

"Ah, here we are," Harry said, suddenly whisking her off the main street and down another mysterious cobbled lane.

Ahead she could see the lights of a pub – from the sound of it, a busy one.

"The famous – nay, infamous – Lamb and Flag," said Harry. "Prepare yourself to meet dear old Alfie."

HARRY spotted Alfie immediately, though the smoke-filled pub was jammed. Not ideal for a quiet chat.

"There he is. Corner table, and using his infamous 'glower' to keep those two seats safe from the horde."

Harry sliced his way through the crowd, pints and cigarettes in their hands, a gauntlet of the six o'clock hour in one of London's best.

Closer, and Alfie looked up, his pug-like face broadening into a smile.

He looked back at Kat who trailed only inches behind him.

Whatever will she make of this man, rough edges and all? Harry thought.

In moments, he'd know.

"HARRY," Alfie said, standing, not on his account, Harry knew – they were way past any "Sir" formalities – but certainly, for Kat.

"Alfie, my friend, may I present to you my wife, Lady Mortimer—"

But Kat wasted no time cutting him off, taking a chair, and Alfie's hand.

"Kat will do just fine," she said with a big smile. "Pleased to meet you, Alfie."

Alfie shot a look, grinning to Harry.

At the smile, the accent? he wondered.

And Harry had to remember exactly where Kat came from.

Having helped her dad run the Lucky Shamrock in the Bronx – right on Broadway, as the great road trailed its way into the countryside – no question she'd be totally comfortable here.

"What are we drinking?" Alfie said.

Harry remained standing.

"If I can fight my way back to the bar, three pints of mild?"

And, as if they were lifelong chums, Alfie and Kat looked up, all smiles, nodding.

KAT TOOK a sip of her warm beer (*still getting used to that*) and studied Alfie as he talked.

Office worker's suit, shirt and tie – faded, but clean. Creases where they should be.

But she could sense that Alfie wasn't quite at ease in such clothes.

Hands like baseball mitts. Face with deep folds and pouches. A man who liked his drink. With that ruddy face, and the hands, you could see he did his share of hard work.

His shoulders and neck, pretty densely packed with muscle.

Tough character, she decided.

One that Harry trusted completely.

LONDON CALLING!

He had told her how Alfie had served with him in the war in France, watched his back as both of them got out of some dangerous scrapes together.

Then, after the war, Alfie had apparently fallen on hard times and paid for some bad choices with a prison stretch. When they reunited after a few years, Harry had helped him get a steady job.

But, as Harry had said, with Alfie's "connections", nobody knew what was happening in London better than he did.

She watched as he took a big draught of his pint, wiping his lips and bristly moustache afterwards.

"So, Harry, glad you're back in old Blighty. But you said you needed my help?"

"Do believe so, old chum. Kat…"

At that, Kat pulled out the photo of Lizzie Spence and slid it to Alfie, while Harry told him of the girl running away, and disappearing in London.

KAT SAW that Alfie held the photo carefully, as if the small black and white image was fragile.

"Bad show," he said, his eyes going from her, then to Harry. "Not that uncommon, these days. The things that get into the heads of young people. And the two of you? Trying to help?"

Harry nodded, then the slightest glance to Kat.

"What we were hoping, Alfie, was that you might ask around. Maybe your, um, mates, people you know? See if they have any idea where such a girl might end up?"

Alfie's face was grim, taking the task seriously.

"Okay. You know, Harry – and you too, Kat – I'd do *anything* to help." He gave the photo a gentle wave. "You say you've checked out all the big theatres?"

Kat nodded.

"Not a sign of her. Which leaves the… smaller places. You know, Alfie, I'm from New York and—"

"New York?" He stared out of the window for a moment. "Now, that is *one* place I would love to go to. Tell me, is it really like you see in the moving pictures? So big… the buildings… all those people?"

Kat laughed. "Why, yes, it is."

"I got to get myself there."

"I'm sure you will, Alfie," she said, smiling and taking a sip of her beer. "So, when I worked in New York. There were bars, nightclubs that – with prohibition – only the locals knew about. Speakeasies. Guess it's the same here?"

"Places like that? Yeah – I can think of a few," said Alfie, "not a million miles from here."

"You could check them out for us?" said Kat.

Harry quickly added, "Can you give it a try, old friend?"

And the slow nod of Alfie's head showed he was on board.

"I will. Tonight even. Nothing else in the diary!"

At that, Alfie produced a low laugh. "And I'll tell you what." Kat watched as Alfie took another long sip of his beer. "I'll put the word out too. Quietly, mind you. You know how it is – Soho, West End. Everybody in these parts knows everybody."

"Appreciate it," Harry said.

"You work around here, Alfie?" said Kat.

"Here and there," said Alfie.

The man coy, as a reflex.

"What kind of line of work are you in?" she said. "If I might ask?"

She saw Harry smiling at her as she attempted to engage, even press Alfie.

LONDON CALLING!

"Oh… Bit of this, bit of that," he said, smiling.

Kat laughed.

"You know, Kat. I can never keep up with Alfie's employment status," said Harry, smiling. "But he always *tells* me it's legitimate."

"The straight and narrow path. Too right, Harry," said Alfie, laughing, placing his hand on his heart, "on my mother's life."

Harry laughed as well, then nodded towards Alfie's empty glass. "Get you another one?"

"Kind of you, Harry, but I'd best be off." Then he leaned in, spoke quietly. "You know, these dancers… When things don't pan out, they can end up in bad places, doing bad things." A last slug of beer. "With bad people."

Alfie let that hang in the air for a moment.

Kat's voice was low. The smoky pub full.

"That's what worries me, Alfie. But I know you'll help."

Another serious nod from Alfie.

"That I will Kat. That I *will*."

At that, Alfie pushed back for the table and stood up.

A solid looking man indeed.

"My mates – they might act a bit cagey. Don't want to get bad people riled, right? You never know."

"That is true, Alfie, you never do," Harry said.

"But they trust me."

Alfie grabbed his hat from a nearby peg and pulled it low, shading his eyes.

"Meet up tomorrow? At the flat?" Harry said.

Alfie nodded.

"Have a good evening," he said, tipping his hat. And with that, he slipped away, disappearing into the crowd as if he'd never existed.

"He's right, you know!" Harry said. "We *do* have the evening before us. Dinner and drinks, I think, don't you?"

"Definitely. Until we get a lead there's not much we can do."

And Harry was up.

"Let me locate the landlord's phone, see if I can book us a table. You, meanwhile," Harry said as he started to move away in search of a telephone, "enjoy the scenery."

As Harry vanished, Kat sat alone at the table with her beer, quite anonymous in the busy crowd.

And very much enjoying the scene. All of it so very *English!*

7.

A NIGHT ON THE TOWN

Harry helped Kat out of the cab and paid off the driver with a good tip.

"Thank you kindly, sir," said the driver as he pulled away, leaving the street in near silence.

Kat put one hand on his shoulder and he watched as she slipped off her shoes, her black silk dress shimmering in the soft street lamps.

"Heels!" she said, holding them aloft. "I hate heels! I mean, how can women wear them all day long? It's torture!"

"Oh, I don't know," he said, watching her spin around, barefoot on the pavement.

Then she put her arm through his as they took the steps together to the main doors of the mansion block.

"Home sweet home," he said, his hat now tucked under his other arm.

"And that lovely bed," said Kat. "I cannot wait. I ate too much. I drank too much. Oh! And – do I remember right – we danced too?"

"Just a little," said Harry, slipping off his dress gloves, and fumbling for his door key.

"With you?" said Kat, nestling into him.

"With me. And with Max."

"Yes. The lovely Max," said Kat. "Surprisingly light on his feet for such a rotund little man. I like him. You must tell me everything about him tomorrow."

"I will," said Harry, smiling. "Old Max – a man of many talents. And I took careful note of his every word."

Kat grinned at that.

And Harry thought how he loved Kat like this.

Carefree, fun. Just about perfect.

One minute talking her head off, and then – guaranteed – a second after her head hit the pillow she'd be fast asleep.

He opened the door and flicked the light on as Kat went ahead of him and pressed the button to summon the lift. The entire block of flats *so* quiet – no surprise, he thought, it must be nearly one o'clock.

Dinner in the Berkeley Grill had been a cosy affair, but then in the bar they'd bumped into a crowd of old pals from his London days.

Everyone had insisted on showing Kat their favourite Mayfair watering holes.

Obviously smitten, he thought, *with his American bride.*

Ending with many champagne flutes at the Ritz courtesy of Max Schultz, Harry's dear friend from an early posting in Berlin back in '20.

Max, it seemed, had given up the diplomatic life to become something of an impresario, opening a string of clubs and theatres across Germany.

And now, here he was in London having the same success. Many champagnes in, he'd insisted he would help Lizzie Spence if they could find her.

"Can't make this silly thing work," said Kat, now leaning against the lift door, prodding the button. "How about we just walk up?"

He turned to shut the front doors, but, as he did, some instinct made him look across the street...

... to see a figure quickly step back from the street light into the shadows.

A man, in a dark trench coat, hat pulled low.

Gone in a flash.

Harry stepped out again onto the pavement and peered down the street. The man had simply *disappeared.*

But there was no question. Whoever it was, he'd been watching Harry. And Kat.

"What is it?" said Kat, joining him. And he could see she was alert now, not at all tipsy.

Like a real pro, he thought.

"Harry – something wrong?"

"Not sure. Not to worry you, but..." he looked at her, "I think – somebody's watching us."

"Really? Well, you know what? That's a good thing."

"It is?" said Harry.

"Someone watching, at this hour. Outside our flat? Means whatever we're doing, we're doing something right."

"You are too clever," he said, nodding. "I agree."

"Come on then, soldier," said Kat, taking his arm again. "Best we get some sleep. Another full day tomorrow. What's the line from your beloved character? Appears that *the game is afoot."*

"Does, doesn't it?"

And he shut the door, its heavy locks reassuring, and walked with her up the stairs to the first floor and their apartment.

KAT KNEW she was dreaming.

One of those moments when you realise *this is a dream*, and yet it rolls on.

She was back in New York at the Lucky Shamrock, but dressed as a can-can dancer, like it was one of those Western movies. Harry was a gunslinger at a table, playing cards with her new pal Max Schultz. Looking like a gambler – pearl-handled revolver in a holster.

Oh, and her dad, grinning, playing the piano.

Alive.

Which is odd, she thought, half-waking, *because Dad doesn't play the piano.*

She turned over in bed, put her hand across the pillow towards Harry, but then – *no dream this!* – he wasn't there.

Now she woke.

She could see light under the bedroom door.

She sat up, listened.

From the other room – voices.

Harry's voice, and another man, speaking low. Trying not to wake her.

She flicked the bedside light on, got up, pulled her silk dressing gown around her, opened the door, and went down the short corridor into the sitting room.

Harry turned quickly as soon as she entered.

"Kat," he said, "didn't want to wake you. You were out for the count."

He was sitting, in his dressing gown, with Alfie at the table.

"Sorry to turn up so late," said Alfie.

"Not a problem," said Kat, walking over to Harry and resting her hand on his shoulder. "You got something for us, Alfie?"

She saw Alfie nod. "Think so. Was just telling Harry here."

LONDON CALLING!

"Seems our Lizzie may have been spotted in a nightclub in Soho," said Harry.

"Can't guarantee," said Alfie. "I mean, without seeing her myself next to that photo. But, by all accounts, it's her all right."

"Nightclub?" said Kat, fearing the worst.

She saw Harry and Alfie exchange a look – both knowing what she meant.

"Place called the Red Rabbit," said Alfie. "New one on me, but word is it's got a reputation."

"Red Rabbit?" said Harry. "Think I can guess what kind of reputation – and it's not veterinary care."

"And Alfie – when was she seen?" said Kat.

"Tonight."

Kat looked over at the clock above the fireplace: two o'clock.

"A place like that – still open, you think?" she said.

"That's why I came over, straight away," said Alfie. "Reckon there's a good hour until it closes."

Kat turned to Harry. "So – what are we waiting for?"

She saw Alfie's expression – a confused look to Harry – then back at Kat. "We?" he said.

Kat laughed. "Think I'm going to let you two have *all* the fun? Come on, Harry – let's get dressed and go."

She saw Harry turn and smile at Alfie.

"What did I tell you?" he said.

Kat raised her eyebrows to Alfie, "Yes, Alfie – what exactly *did* he tell you?"

"Um… he said the moment you knew about the club he wouldn't be able to hold you back."

"He wouldn't even try," said Kat, smiling at Harry, then she headed back to the bedroom to get dressed.

At last, she thought, *a real lead.*

The fog created by the champagne suddenly, excitingly, vanished.

KAT SQUEEZED in next to Harry on the front seat of Alfie's old Austin truck, and, with a crunch of gears, they headed off down Bedford Avenue, the streets now totally empty.

The night was cool and she was glad of the slacks she'd packed. When they were on a case, she and Harry each threw an extra bag in the car: not quite disguises, but old clothes, jackets, boots, caps.

And tonight they were coming in handy. She looked across at Harry – in a tattered suit and cardigan, mismatched trousers and scuffed shoes; he looked like an impoverished clerk, someone totally down on their luck.

He was sporting an old pair of horn-rimmed spectacles, and his Brylcremed, parted hair completed the look.

Alfie didn't need to change, his clothes magically seemed to suit every occasion.

She looked out of the truck window at the London streets as they crossed Oxford Street and drove deep into Soho. Every place was now long shut, though the big hotels were still brightly lit as they passed.

A few pedestrians remained, and taxis whisked the tipsy wealthy home after their late nights out. She could see the occasional cop – or "bobby" as Harry called them – on his beat, standing in shadows, or on street corners.

Now the streets narrowed, past tiny stores, boarded up cafés, workshops, little apartments, she guessed.

Nothing like this in Manhattan, she thought.

"Here we are. Lexington Street," said Alfie, as he took a turn. The truck's wheels clattered on the cobbled stones, and Kat peered out. This little backstreet had no street lamps.

Just the faint light from a moon above, under scudding clouds.

"So. All know what we're doing?" said Harry.

"Yes," said Kat and Alfie together.

"Good, good."

They'd made a quick plan back in the flat. Kat on lookout duty in the truck. Alfie and Harry would do the *recce*.

Alfie slowed, then pulled in onto one side of the street, up on the pavement.

He turned the engine off. They waited for a minute in silence, but it seemed nobody had taken notice of their arrival.

"Okay. Club's down there on the left," said Alfie. "Basement entrance. Two doors: one's a kind of stage door, I guess – the other's the way in."

"I don't see a sign," said Kat.

"Ha! Place isn't legal," said Alfie. "So no flashing neon Red Rabbit! A double knock on the door gets us in."

"We ready?" said Harry. "Kat – you okay here?"

Kat nodded as she watched them both climb out. Then she slid across into the driver's seat – with the fervent hope she wouldn't have to actually drive this creaky, lumbering truck.

"This time of night, I don't think anyone will take any note of you out here," said Harry quietly, leaning in to the open driver's window. "But Kat. Listen. Anything happens, just hit the gas and go, right? If you're not here when we get out – rendezvous back at the flat."

"Gotcha," said Kat, feeling a bit frustrated that she wasn't coming into the club. But still, loving being on watch out here – the night alive with the tension of being back on a live case.

Time was, back in her days working for the US government, she'd worked surveillance herself, in some tight spots.

None of it in the government's job description, but exactly what she had been trained to do.

She knew Harry was only slowly beginning to realise the full extent of her résumé from that time.

One not so different from his own.

"Don't have too much fun," she said, reaching out to adjust his spectacles.

"Spoilsport," said Harry, kissing the tip of his finger and putting it gently to her lips. He gave her a wink, then turned, put a friendly arm around Alfie's shoulder, and the two of them sauntered off down the street.

To a casual observer, just a couple of tipsy old mates looking for a little extra fun to round off a wild night on the town.

Kat leaned back into her seat and slid down, until she knew her face was lost in shadow.

Her whole body alert to the sight and sound of this hundred-yard stretch of London street.

LONDON CALLING!

8.

THE RED RABBIT CLUB

Harry gave a nod to Alfie, then slipped ahead of him down unlit narrow steps that led from the street to the front door of the Red Rabbit Club.

He could see nothing on the heavy metal door that indicated what might lie on the inside.

Just a small panel, the size of a book, in the centre of the door.

He knocked firmly on the door – two sharp knocks. After a few seconds, the panel slid open and a pair of eyes appeared. Harry saw the eyes flick from him to Alfie and up the steps to the street.

Then the panel slammed shut and, a second later, the door popped open to reveal a short, squat man with a hewn and weary face, and hands the size of dinner plates.

Harry watched as the man shuffled to one side – been a long night, Harry guessed – and nodded them in, his eyes tiny black beads in his broad head.

Harry followed as Alfie went past him, into a small dark ante-room, draped with heavy dark-red curtains on all the walls. He heard the door shut behind them.

Another man, tall in a faded dress suit and silver spats, stepped forward, his words more of a bark than the King's English.

"Table charge. Ten bob each. Pay now. Gets you one drink each. Bar's open until three. One more show to come, but no talking to the girls. The two of yers got that?"

Harry reached into his pocket and pulled out a thick wad of notes, purposely flashed, taking his time; the bills culled earlier from his wallet and wrapped carefully around a core of old newspaper.

But in the shadows it looked like *quite a roll*, he knew.

"There's ten shillings," he said. Then he peeled off another note. "Oh – and an extra ten for a good table?"

"Oh – certainly, sir!" said the man, his demeanour shifting instantly at the sight of the roll of banknotes. "Pleasure to have *yous* here tonight."

Good, thought Harry. *Taking me for a sucker, as Kat would call it.*

All set to be fleeced.

He slipped the roll of "cash" back in his pocket.

"This way, sir, *please*," said the man, pulling aside one of the heavy drapes and opening a door that lay behind it.

Harry thought the club would be deserted. He wasn't expecting the blast of noise, pounding jazz music, swirling cigarette smoke and red lights which hit him as he stepped through into the club. The place was packed!

He looked round at Alfie, behind him, who likewise seemed astonished. The two of them over the years – going back even to wartime France – had been in some interesting late-night bars and dives, but Harry had to admit, *this was something*.

Maybe twenty tables spread in an arc around a small stage, in front of which a four-piece jazz band was playing loudly. The crowd – mostly men, but with a handful of women – were crammed around the tables, drinking, laughing, the loud blaring music ignored.

Harry could see more revellers pressed against a bar that ran the length of one wall, the mirrored wall behind lined with bottles of spirits. Turning the other way, he saw more men surrounding a roulette table.

Not strictly a gambling joint, but clearly – in the Rabbit – anything goes that brings in money, he thought.

As Harry and Alfie were led through the smoky club to an empty table just by the stage, Harry took in the clientele. They were a real cross-section of London: a handful of men in full evening dress, wealthy toffs looking as if they'd come from Mayfair parties; others in lounge suits; a few even in working men's jackets.

The atmosphere – illicit, exotic, underground. A melting pot of classes, drawn by the booze, the music.

And, Harry guessed, *the show to come.*

The few women – all accompanied by what looked like big spenders – were mostly in their twenties and flashily dressed. It didn't look to Harry like any of them were paying guests who'd arrived with the men.

The age discrepancy alone ruled that out.

He and Alfie took their seats, and Harry slipped another note into their host's hand. "Champagne!" he said.

"Of course, sir," said the man.

"Champagne?" said Alfie, as the man scurried away. "Half a mild would have done me."

"Oh, do come on, Alfie. All part of the act tonight, eh?" said Harry, adjusting his spectacles. "Little man from out of town suddenly wins big at the races – money to throw away."

"Right. Guess I'll just have to suffer," said Alfie.

They both turned at a loud pop behind them – to see their bottle of champagne being poured.

"The last show will start in five minutes, sir," said the man.

"Can't wait," said Harry. Then he raised his glass to Alfie. "Here's to the dancing girls. And may they be *everything* we're expecting."

KAT SAT in the darkness of the truck cab, watching.

She'd seen quite a number of men going into and out of the club, mostly in small groups. Despite the hour, the place was still clearly busy.

Whatever were Harry and Alfie getting up to inside?

She'd certainly drawn the short straw – though she knew if she'd gone with them it might have complicated the little routine they'd planned.

Best they play two "blokes", suddenly flush with cash.

She'd only complicate the tale.

Then, she heard the sound of a door opening ahead and saw a bar of light briefly illuminate the street. A figure climbed the steps, from what she guessed was the stage door, onto the street.

A bear of a man – looking as wide as he was tall.

She watched as he lit a cigarette, flicked the match away and stared up and down the street as if he owned it.

Then – a chilling moment – as his eyes seemed to fix on her truck and she saw the cigarette glow red as he took a deep drag.

And, as if he'd made up his mind that something wasn't quite right, he started walking…

… in her direction.

Uh-oh, she thought. *What's my cover story?*

Um… I'm doing a vegetable delivery and I got here a tad early? Maybe… my husband's out on the town somewhere and he asked me to pick him up?

It occurred to Kat that they'd skipped that part of the story.

Or tell the truth? But no, that wouldn't fly, not with Harry and Alfie under cover in there.

She sank lower in the seat, trying to *think*. The man was still twenty yards away. If she started the truck now – *if it started first time* – she could just pull out and drive away.

Like Harry said.

Heart pounding, she reached down and fumbled for the key in the unfamiliar vehicle. Through the windshield she could see the man just ten yards away now.

As he kept on coming.

He had to be able to see her now.

Her fumbling fingers finally found the key, grasped it. She started to turn it, when, behind the man, the side door to the club opened again. A shaft of light on the cobbled street, and a voice ringing out.

"Charlie? Where the *hell* are you? Charlie!"

Kat swallowed, waited and watched – held her breath as the man stopped dead, turned.

"All right," he shouted in the direction of the door, voice echoing on the empty street. "Keep yer bloody 'air on!"

Then he flipped the stub of his cigarette away, and walked back towards the Red Rabbit Club.

Kat let her breath out.

"Phew," she said, opening the truck window for some fresh air.

Her fingers released their hold on the truck's ignition key.

Close call.

"LADIES AND GENTLEMEN, put your hands together and give one last late-night welcome to the stars of our show: the beautiful, the mesmerising, the gorgeous, Red Rabbit Belles!"

Harry glanced quickly at Alfie, then back at the stage as the lights dimmed, the band played an intro, and the raucous crowd cheered, their attention finally on the small stage area.

And then, giddily shuffling onto the stage in a line, came the dancers: all spangly, with diamond sparkling headdresses, red heels, and matching red "fur" costumes that left little to the imagination.

There were four of them – and they spread out and kicked into their routine, not exactly with the precision of the "Ziegfeld Follies". But, all things considered, not too bad.

Harry quickly scanned their faces. Two blondes, two brunettes, all looking to be in their thirties if not older.

The kicks high, but their eyes… looking distracted.

And not young!

Lizzie Spence was just twenty-one.

For a second, he was disappointed. All this - another wild goose chase. He looked over at Alfie.

"She's not here," said Harry.

"Wait," said Alfie. Harry saw him nod to the far side of the stage.

"Take a look. One at the end," he said.

Harry, confused, followed Alfie's glance, and looked again at the fourth dancer.

And the more he looked, the more he realised.

This dancer *wasn't* in her thirties. Up close now, he could see: make-up plastered on, tight wig obscuring her own hair, the costume something he'd never associated with that old photograph.

There was no doubt about it.

LONDON CALLING!

The tall blonde dancer on stage – high kicking to catcalls from the front tables – was Lizzie Spence

9.

LOST

The performance lasted only twenty minutes, though – as Harry explained to Kat later – *"it was very… um… spirited"*.

The second the dancers finished, the curtain unceremoniously dropped and they were gone. The band kicked off on a last jazzy number and the calls of "encore" quickly fizzled out.

When their host in the patent shoes came to top up their champagne, Harry had a question.

"Um, I say, old chap. I wonder if any of the girls could join us for a drink?"

The man froze for a second. Looked at the two of them.

Evaluating us? Harry thought. *Or perhaps our financial resources?*

"Oh dear me, no, sir," said the man. "We're really not *that* kind of club, I'm sure sir understands?"

Harry shrugged.

The Red Rabbit might not be that kind of club – but it didn't look far off it. Harry guessed for the right customer, anything was possible.

When the man had gone, he leaned in to Alfie, so they could talk over the loud music.

"Going to see if I can slip round the back," he said. "Keep your eyes open."

"Got it, chief," said Alfie – those three words always reassuring to Harry.

Harry got up and threaded his way through the busy tables, past the bar and stage towards a sign that indicated the WCs.

Next to it, he saw a swing door that probably led to the rooms and offices behind.

Maybe to the dressing rooms?

With a quick glance to check nobody was watching, he slipped through the swing door to find himself in a corridor, with another corridor leading from it in the direction of the back of the stage.

It was quieter back here, the music muted.

As he stood orienting himself, a door ahead opened. Quickly he backed into a corner and pressed against the side of a cupboard. Two men in scruffy dinner jackets walked past and into the club without seeing him.

Harry peered round the cupboard and listened.

Coast clear.

He walked down the corridor and turned into the next one. He could see the doors were marked "Manager", "Props", "Stores" – then finally a door tagged "Dressing Rooms".

Bingo!

He stepped up close to the door. From inside he could hear voices – female – the dancers chattering away.

Another look up and down the corridor: empty.

He tapped on the door.

"Cor! Five minutes, Charlie, don't you bloody listen?" came an irritated voice from inside.

Harry knocked again.

After a few seconds, it opened and one of the dancers stood there, still in costume. "Charlie Leet, we're not your bloody–?" said the woman, confused at the sight of Harry, not the expected Charlie. "Who the hell are you?" she said.

"Hello," said Harry in his most timid voice.

"Where's Charlie? You don't—"

"Oh, gosh. Terribly sorry," said Harry, playing the nervous out-of-towner. "Don't want to disturb. Um. Charlie said I could drop by. Said it was fine."

"Oh yeah?" said the woman, laughing. "What do you want then… young man?"

"Want? Oh, um, well. I'm just… a fan. Art of the dance, you know? Think you're marvellous. All of you. Wanted to say thank you. Perhaps, perhaps… buy you all a drink?" He took a breath, "Or something?" He looked left and right, as if concerned about his next words. "I mean, got all these winnings burning a hole in my pocket, you know?"

The woman looked at Harry as if deciding whether she believed him. Then she laughed as she pulled the door open wider.

Now Harry could peer in, and he saw the two blonde dancers leaning against dressing tables, also still in costume, smoking.

And – sitting to one side, looking weary, and alone – *Lizzie Spence, wig off, wiping at the make-up on her face.*

She didn't look up – just stared down at the floor.

"What's up, Peggy?" said one of the blonde women.

"Fella here says he wants to buy us a 'drink', girls," said the woman. "Blimey – we never had *that* offer before!"

The women laughed.

"Let's see the colour of his money then," shouted one of the other dancers, walking over and joining the first at the door.

The first dancer looked Harry up and down. "If he's got any!"

"Money?" said Harry, blinking. "Oh yes, money."

He dug into his trouser pocket, then tugged out his wad of "cash".

"Look!" he said. "I guess I just got lucky! On the gee-gees, you know... the horses!"

"Did you *now*?" came a deep voice from behind him.

Harry spun round – just as a gnarled hand grabbed his wrist like a claw. The owner – the squat man who'd been at the club door.

Charlie Leet, I presume, thought Harry.

"Ow!" said Harry. "You know, um, that hurts!"

"This man here bothering you, Pegs?" said the man, still holding Harry's wrist tight.

Harry yelped as realistically as he could – and made a mental note that before this case was over he would return the favour to Charlie Leet – with interest.

"Ha," said Peggy. "Look at 'im! Doubt he could bother anything."

"Lost, are we?" said Leet, pressing his pockmarked face close to Harry's.

"Right! Must have taken the wrong turning," said Harry with a gulp. "Then I thought, why not offer to buy these good ladies a drink."

He watched as Leet prised the roll of cash from his hand.

"Did you now?" he said. "Very gentlemanly of you."

Harry saw him peel a couple of notes from the roll, and slip them into his trouser pocket.

"Tell you what. Bar's about to close. So why don't I buy those drinks on your behalf, eh? And in return – I won't say a word to the management about you loitering back here harassing these... vulnerable... young girls. Gotta tell you, mate, the boss doesn't take kindly to such things."

70

He took the rest of the wad – only a few notes shy of revealing the newspaper within – and jammed it into Harry's jacket pocket. Harry saw the women laugh.

"How does that sound, *pal?*" said Leet giving Harry's wrist one last squeeze, then letting it go. "Reasonable?"

"Oh yes," said Harry, rubbing his crushed wrist. "Jolly reasonable, indeed."

Leet put his hands on Harry's shoulders, and turned him round so he pointed back into the club.

"Now off you go, young man," said Leet. "And we'll both forget this ever happened."

Speak for yourself, thought Harry.

He started to shuffle slowly back along the corridor. Behind him he heard Leet talking to the women.

"You ready, girls? Don't want to keep the boss waiting, now, do we?"

He glanced back over his shoulder to see the dancers now filing out behind Charlie, coats draped over their shoulders.

Lizzie Spence, last of the group.

So, they were going to see the "boss".

At this hour?

Didn't sound good.

Harry knew there was no way he and Alfie could pay the bill and get out onto the street in time to follow them.

But Kat was out there.

And knowing Kat... *she would handle it.*

KAT SAW a sleek, black sedan pull up outside the club – and was immediately on the alert. All the time she'd been on lookout, not a single vehicle had stopped in the narrow street.

LONDON CALLING!

She watched as the car stood there, engine idling, waiting.

Then the stage door opened again. She leaned forward in her seat to get a better view.

First the big guy came up the steps, stopped, checked the street, then went to the sedan, said something through the passenger window.

Then he turned back, gestured down to the stage door. And now Kat saw a line of women emerge, coats over their shoulders, not even close to disguising the shimmer and sparkle of their costumes.

Dancers. Four of them.

A rear door in the sedan opened – and the women piled in.

The big guy shut the car door, then, with one last look up and down the street, he heaved himself into the front passenger seat and shut that door too.

Then the sedan pulled away from the club and headed down Lexington Street.

Kat glanced back at the club. No sign of Harry and Alfie.

Quick thoughts racing through her head.

The girls, the dancers... she couldn't make anything out.

But was one Lizzie Spence?

And if so, where was she being taken?

Harry had been inside long enough for Kat to know he must have hit pay-dirt. If Lizzie hadn't been in there, they would have been out straight away.

One of those four women had to be Lizzie.

And Kat *had* to follow them.

Quickly, she started the truck – *thank God for electric starters* – took a guess at first gear, released the handbrake, and without turning on the lights at first, drove after the dancers, the lumbering truck rocking on the cobblestone street.

She saw the black car ahead, shoot across the first junction, and Kat crunched through the unfamiliar gears, gaining speed, trying to catch up.

The streets totally deserted – too late for revellers, still too early for the first workers of the new day.

Ahead, she saw the car take a sharp right. She followed, not knowing what these streets were, or which direction she was heading towards.

Was the driver aware he had a truck on his tail?

And if not, what would happen if he spotted her?

She followed, and with another turn she suddenly realised, to her relief, she *knew* where she was.

Ahead – one of London's best-known landmarks: Piccadilly Circus, the statue of Eros lit with gloomy street lights.

This time of night, all the advertising lights turned off, the theatre displays dark.

Around the statue, and down Piccadilly she drove, her foot flat down trying to get some speed out of Alfie's old truck.

Just hours ago, she and Harry had walked this grand avenue with his pals, stopping for champagne cocktails in various hotel bars.

Now she was driving an old Austin pickup – fast as it could go, which wasn't fast at all – in pursuit of a runaway girl in a suspicious sedan.

On her right she saw a building, noting the sign quickly: the Royal Academy. Then, in a blur of speed on her left, the Ritz, the hotel's doorman, in top hat and tails, still on duty.

Past Berkeley Street now – the sedan ahead, the only car on the empty streets. Suddenly, she saw it take a sharp right.

She followed, tyres screeching at the quick turn – just missing a cab that appeared from nowhere, its horn tooting angrily at her.

LONDON CALLING!

Down a narrow street of tall houses, the sedan just visible ahead, taking a left and going out of sight.

It would be so easy to lose it on these streets, she knew.

Still she followed, missing a gear and feeling the rear of the truck beginning to twitch and slide, gears groaning before she managed to correct the drift.

She could again see the car a hundred yards ahead. It took another right.

Jeez, these streets! she thought, her sweating hands pulling at the heavy steering wheel. *No logic to them!*

Give me Manhattan's orderly grid!

Suddenly in front of her – bang in the middle of the street, hand aloft – a policeman!

She hit the brakes, the truck sliding to a grinding, noisy halt just feet away from him.

She saw the policeman lower his hand and shake his head.

Behind him, at the far end of the street, the sedan took another turn and disappeared from view.

"Damn," she said quietly, as if the officer could hear her.

But the cop walked slowly over to her window, a mythic figure with his tall bobby's hat.

"I don't care if you're late to market, mate – there's no call for that kind of speed." Then he clearly saw that it was a woman driving. "Oh," he said.

"Evening officer," said Kat. "I can explain…"

"I'm sure you can, madam," said the cop. "This time of night? I'm all ears."

"A PRANK?" said Harry, handing Kat a coffee and a plate of toast, then joining her on the sofa.

He saw her nod and then watched as she took a sip of the drink.

"Gosh, I needed that," she said.

"And our London bobby… he believed you?"

"I'm a very honest looking woman, Harry," she said, leaning back against the cushions, suddenly feeling exhausted.

"'Bewitching' is the word, I believe," he said, smiling at her. "I expect he wasn't immune to that."

He waited, while she devoured a slice of toast.

"So," she said, mouth still full. "Dead end, you talking to Lizzie at the club. And dead end, me finding out the mysterious destination of that sedan."

"Unfortunately," said Harry. "From what I saw of her – Lizzie didn't look happy."

"Not surprised, working a joint like that. You didn't get even a hint where the girls were being taken?"

"To the boss – that's all I heard."

"Doesn't sound good, does it?" said Kat. "You know, if she were my daughter, I'd go in fighting and not come out till I had her safe."

"I know you would. Though I suspect there's no shortage of heavies in that place."

"But Harry – you said you had a plan?"

"I do," said Harry, stealing a piece of her toast. "It does involve some, um, special assistance from you, though."

"And?"

"I wonder," he said. "Remember you told me you were something of a dancer, back in the day?"

He watched her carefully, as she put down her toast mid-mouthful.

"Yes…" she said.

And – taking a breath, because what he was about to suggest was somewhat outlandish – he told her the plan he'd come up with.

10.

SHOWTIME

Harry, with Alfie trailing behind, found that they were immediately led to their table from the night before, a prime spot at the Red Rabbit to take in the show.

And even before they had sat down, the grinning waiter from their previous visit had materialised, his smile less about seeing old customers back for more, than anticipating the wad of notes that Harry seemed to have dispensed so easily.

"Two champagnes?" the waiter said.

But this time Harry shot a look at Alfie, that rumpled face not always revealing what was going on inside the chiselled brow under his close-cropped haircut.

"Um, yes, but I think my friend here—"

Alfie finished the sentence. "Pint of mild will do me fine."

The waiter – though perhaps disappointed with an order of beer – nonetheless kept his smile plastered on as he said, "Absolutely!" and whisked away to the bar area.

Harry looked at his watch.

"Just a few minutes now."

At that, Alfie leaned forward. "Didn't want to worry you, Harry. But spoke to some other people today. You know, asked around."

Harry nodded, as the champagne flute and pint arrived. Harry peeled off a note and waved the waiter away.

"Yes. And what exactly did you hear?" Harry took a sip.

Truth be told, he wasn't overly fond of champagne. Under the right circumstances, with the right person, well then… *of course.*

But now he would have liked nothing more than a large whisky. Still… *when in Rome.*

"They say, the people behind this joint," Alfie waved his bear-claw of a hand, "are not people to be *messin'* with."

"I was rather getting that impression myself. Nevertheless, what you did this afternoon? Neatly done. Brilliant, in fact. As to what happens now…"

"Anything goes?"

"Well, let's hope not 'anything'. But we'd best be ready."

"Oh, I'm ready, chief."

At that, Alfie patted the side pocket of his jacket.

Alfie, Harry knew, was one of those types who was always ready.

If things got tough – well, whatever he had packed away in that side pocket could prove mighty useful.

And, at that, the small jazz band blared out a noisy tune, full of energy but – in Harry's opinion – lacking any finesse.

The master of ceremonies popped onto the stage, grinning at the room full of people. Business at the Rabbit was good.

"Ladies…"

Harry looked around. This night, he didn't see any "ladies" out among the sea of men.

Well, presumably the MC had a script to follow.

"… and gentlemen. The Red Rabbit is proud to present…" The MC began backing away to the side, gesturing stage left. "The Red Rabbit Belles!"

A smattering of applause greeted the overenthusiastic announcement. The curtain started chugging upward, and, as soon as it was up, out came the dancers.

With the one on the extreme right, gamely following all the moves and steps…

Harry's own wife – Kat.

Or – as she was more formally known, back in Sussex – *Lady Katherine Mortimer, in-law of Lady Lavinia Fitzhenry of Mydworth Manor.*

And, for a moment, all Harry could do was just watch.

Spellbound.

KAT WASN'T completely surprised that the squat bulldog of a man, who seemed to be in charge of the day-to-day running of the club, had said she could start that night.

After all, he was down one dancer. That dancer, as far as the club knew, was at home sick. In reality she'd been paid five pounds by Alfie to "take the evening off". And after Kat had insisted that she was indeed well trained, a quick learner, and with her big smile hopefully radiating American pluckiness, he'd told her to come that afternoon for rehearsals and run-throughs.

But now, as she shuffled with the other girls, the choreography basic but still a challenge, she kept a smile on her face, even as her eyes dotted right to check she was doing something approaching the correct steps.

And when the girls linked arms and began high kicking, well, Kat handled all that with ease. Whistles from the audience greeting those kicks to the stratosphere.

She realised that she was more than keeping up – at least trajectory wise – with the other dancers.

Every now and then, during the routine, she tried to make out Harry, who she knew had to be sitting out there, in the dark.

God knows what he was thinking, seeing his relatively new wife parading about in the skimpiest of outfits, reflective spangles providing only a hint of modesty.

But the bright spotlights were totally blinding on the stage; the club could have been empty, or filled with shadowy mannequins, the only reassurance that there *was* an audience being the occasional claps and whistles.

Those whistles letting the Red Rabbit Belles know that they weren't exactly performing Shakespeare here.

She glanced along the line of dancers, trying to see the young girl at the end.

Lizzie Spence. Her smile rigidly in place.

Kat had tried to get a few words with her in rehearsal, the point of this whole plan. But with the make-up, feathers, costumes and quick check of the routine, so far there had been no chance for that.

As for the two older dancers – they seemed actively hostile.

Like maybe they suspected the American. Something suspicious in how she got the job?

Showbusiness, Kat thought.

If this was it, she was happy with the career path she had chosen.

"BLIMEY, Harry – I've got to say. Kat? She can *dance*."

"So I was informed. Apparently had a decent amount of training, and even harboured hopes of becoming a professional."

"Damn impressive, I'd say."

"And I must say, Alfie, what an outfit!"

At that Alfie laughed.

"Don't know her all that well yet, boss, but can't imagine she's *enjoying* this, is she?"

"Hard to tell. But if it means we learn something about the young girl, I believe that wife of mine would put up with anything."

The jazz band – sometimes seeming like they were all playing a different piece of music – shifted their rhythm, and now the dancers began a tricky mix of raising their knees, followed by kicks, and spinning in place.

Harry could see, with this added complication, Kat falling behind, the smile on her face definitely turning a bit wobbly.

But, well, with all that rouge and lipstick and the skimpy costumes, it was unlikely the audience had taken note of her grimace.

Harry also guessed that she couldn't see him.

Would love some eye contact, he thought. *Maybe some indication that she's chatted with Lizzie?*

Perhaps even learned something?

But for now, Harry was, in both senses, totally in the dark.

AFTER A roller-coaster set of fifteen minutes that seemed to race by like a train barrelling down the track without a driver, the performance ended, the dancers bowing in unison.

Kat followed the others backstage, the troupe performing – as directed – rather idiotic bunny hops as they left.

She was breathing hard. After all, dancing like this? It had been a while.

The women, weary, silently treading back to the dressing room area.

Kat let the other two dancers – one already popping a cigarette into her mouth – walk ahead, while she drifted back to where Lizzie, as if lingering behind them, moved more slowly.

Now or never, Kat thought.

"Wow," Kat said, "that's one tough routine."

Lizzie looked up. The face set, eyes narrow. *Grim, would be the word.*

"Yeah. It's hard." Then she started to move past Kat.

But Kat didn't let her shuffle too far.

"But you still do it?"

The girl barely looked up. "This place? The punters out there?" her face lit up with sarcasm. "Oh, it's my dream come true."

More steps to the dressing room, but Kat wanted to get in as many questions as she could before being under the scrutiny of the two other dancers.

Doubt they have much sympathy for young Lizzie, Kat guessed.

She risked a touch, reaching for Lizzie's arm.

"Lizzie, right?" The girl at least stopped moving. "Then why don't you just leave?"

And at that, Kat immediately knew – standing in the darkness, still in costume, the spangles barely reflecting the scant light – she'd hit a nerve.

Because the girl took a step closer.

"You're the new girl. Yank, to boot. You don't know *anything*, do you?"

"Well, I—"

"About how things run here? The way things" – long pause – "are."

And in that moment, Kat saw that while Lizzie might barely be twenty-one, something had happened here to make her sound decades older.

Then Kat – again realising that she had to take absolutely any opportunity – said, "Right. I *don't* know. But I want to. I want to understand."

Kat was tempted to say even more. But she held her tongue. That could really backfire, scare the girl.

Because it sounded very much like Lizzie Spence was trapped.

Lizzie waited for a long time, before taking a breath, then said, "Really?" Then she shook her head. "We have to get ready before the next show, don't have time—"

Kat risked another touch to a bare shoulder.

"Maybe later? We can" – a small smile, hoping to disarm her – "talk some more?"

At that, the girl nodded. But whether dismissively or in agreement, Kat couldn't tell.

Lizzie turned and walked away.

The night was only beginning at the Red Rabbit.

11.

SECRETS OF THE RED RABBIT

Harry looked at his watch. It had been a night of shows, and no information from Kat. He and Alfie had long since swapped their beer and bubbly for soda water.

And with the lack of information – *had Kat learned anything?* – they grew silent.

Except, as they headed to the last show of the night, Alfie sniffed the smoke-filled air, played with his glass of water.

"This is hard, chief. Sitting here, not knowing."

Harry nodded – but he knew that whatever happened, would be different from the night before.

The plan: in the middle of the last set, Alfie would go and bring the Alvis round to the front of the club.

No rattling old Austin van to tail the mysterious black car, this time.

That is, *if it even turned up again tonight.*

Harry knew he was pretty good at tailing someone. Staying just far enough back, so in the rear-view mirror his headlights remained small, almost unnoticed. Nothing to be alarmed about.

"Well, Alfie, I think we'll know soon enough."

The band started playing, even less synchronised than before, probably fuelled by the free drinks provided all night.

And Harry sat there, his face set too.

Wondering… *what is happening?*

KAT HAD WAITED until Lizzie had left the dressing room, to turn to one of the other girls. Meg she said her name was.

Kat came close, ignoring the girl's openly disinterested look.

"Um, this place, what they pay you… doesn't exactly cover the rent, does it?"

Meg fired a look at her partner, and took the role of spokesperson.

"Pays enough, I reckon. You used to getting more? For your 'services' back in the States?"

At that, the two hardened dancers laughed.

"Well, no. But was thinking… sometimes I used to, you know, pick up a little bit extra. After a club closes?"

Another look fired between the girls. And Meg took a step towards her as if ready to challenge.

"Oh, right? And how exactly did you do that?"

Eyes fixed on her. Kat decided not to directly attempt to answer that question. Instead, "You girls, know anything here that might bring in some extra cash?"

Meg grinned at this. "Spare bob or two, you mean?"

"Something like that."

And the girl took a breath.

"Maybe. Though, tell *yer* what, girlie. You best talk to old Charlie 'bout that. Me, and Sally here? We don't know nothin'."

Meg turned on her heels.

Only minutes till the next show.

Charlie…

Kat had to take a shot at it, so she spun away and hurried to the door, out of the cramped dressing room, to the corridors, following the stench of stale cigar smoke, to find Charlie Leet.

KAT SAW Leet standing by the stage, sucking on the now unlit cigar stub. Chewing at it.

And she tried to be coy.

But she knew, last night, all the girls packed into that expensive black sedan? They went somewhere.

Charlie would know where. *Why.*

Still, she had to tread cautiously.

"Charlie, I was wondering—"

"*Whatsamatta?* The other dancers? They're not giving you problems are they?"

Then Leet took a small step forward, like a toad hopping one slimy lily pad closer.

"Cause, I tell you, kid. You're looking good, from out front, never know you was just hired."

The cigar stub received a chew or two, as if the chunk of tobacco was part of the conversation.

Kat smiled, concealing the real emotion the tubby troll in front of her summoned.

"Just that, you know, being here in England, money's so tight. One of the girls they mentioned—"

She didn't have to go any further.

"Ah, right. Gotcha. Wanna earn a few extra bob, eh?"

Though she knew the term, Kat decided to continue with the role of parvenu just washed up on foreign shores.

"Bob?"

"Money."

"The other girl, Sally, said—"

Charlie nodded. "Yeah. The after-hours thing?" Charlie looked away as if checking that no one was in earshot. "Bit of a private show, you know? Nice clientele." Again he leaned towards her as he repeated. "*Real* nice. Pretty much what you do here, at the Rabbit, got it? Dancin' and all. But maybe... just a little bit friendlier."

Kat forced a smile and offered what she hoped was a convincing reply: "That sounds great."

And Charlie Leet laughed. "You Yanks, you don't waste no time, do you? Moving in on whatever's going on. Okay, you just be ready to go after the show."

Another grin from Leet. "Transport and the rest of it - all sorted."

Kat nodded as Charlie began to turn away.

"Just one thing," she said. "Um, outside, there's this guy. Guess you'd call him a stage-door Johnny. Wanted to, you know, see me after the show."

Charlie's beady eyes remained locked on her.

"I think I better ask him to just leave. When he's done."

"I could get him to lay off. Don't want the customers messin' with you girls anyway."

Kat gave Charlie another smile. "I mean, the guy, seems nice enough. Maybe, best, you know, I just run out. Tell him?"

And though Kat realised that she hadn't offed any logic for her delivering the message to the imagined swain she was discussing, Charlie nodded.

"I s'pose. Just be quick. Last set coming up. End with a bang." And at that, Charlie laughed as if he had just made one hell of a joke.

"End with a bang – ha!"

And with a nod, he indicated that Kat could dash out to the audience.

Out to Harry.

HARRY SAW Kat emerge from the side door. In seconds she was there. Leaning down.

A rather fabricated grin on her face.

Her voice low.

"Harry – act disappointed okay? But I'm 'in'. After the show."

"What do you mean?" Harry said, his brow furrowed, and no acting at all. Not sure what new step his plan had just taken.

"I'm going to go with the girls, after the last show."

"Kat, I'm not sure—"

But Kat kept smiling at him.

God, he thought, *she could be one excellent actress.*

"It's the only way. Spoke to Lizzie. But she wouldn't talk. Clammed up. This way – think we can find out what's really going on."

But over her shoulder, Harry saw the big guy, Charlie, come out.

"Oh – there's um, dunno, your boss."

"Soon as the show's over, we go. You guys follow. I'll find out what's happening. I'll feel a lot better if I know you have my back covered."

Harry cleared his throat.

"Got it."

He wanted to add that he wasn't pleased with what sounded like both a daring and dangerous addition to the evening's activities. But already he saw Charlie waddling over in the direction of the table.

So instead, he nodded with his best disappointed look. Then his voice equally low.

"I'll be there. Right behind you." *Charlie almost there.* "Be careful."

Kat spun away, hurrying backstage, dodging Charlie in mid-journey to the table.

While Harry busied himself trying to look disappointed.

"Night's not over, Alfie. In fact, it just got a lot more interesting."

"So I heard, chief."

12.

A VERY PRIVATE PARTY

Last show of the night over, Kat noticed that the other women hurried to pack their spangled costumes, stuffing them into small satchels.

Kat followed suit, but her eyes were also locked on Lizzie, who was doing the same thing. But unlike the businesslike way the older dancers went about getting ready, Lizzie moved slowly.

Like someone being forced.

Then a sharp knock. The door opened. Charlie Leet didn't care if the women were still dressing.

"Car's here," he barked. "Get a move on. Shake them legs."

And Kat, like the others, made sure she had her stuff all gathered.

She felt a tinge of fear. What exactly was she about to face?

Just hope Harry has better luck tailing the black sedan than I did!

"OKAY, Alfie. Here they come."

Harry had the Alvis pulled tight to the building.

Engine off, they sat in the shadows.

Harry was close enough to see Leet open the back door of the sedan. As the girls hurried in, Leet looked up and down the street as if moving contraband.

Do the bobbies keep bankers' hours in this part of London? Harry thought.

Couldn't be more deserted.

"Sure you don't want me to take the wheel, Harry? I know these streets. I'm on them all the time."

Harry nodded. A good point from his loyal batman. But then Harry had – for king and country – done quite a few tails; on foot, in a vehicle, and in a lot of exotic locales.

So, as to who'd be better driving in the next few minutes, it was probably a toss-up.

"Thanks Alfie, I think I can handle it. But any hints as we hit the streets, then do pass them along."

The sedan started to roll away from the kerb.

"Here we go," Harry said.

My Kat is in that car. If anything happens to her…

He had a couple of visions of how that could end.

EVERYONE in the car sat deathly quiet.

But Kat's position in the back allowed her to see the driver. His narrow eyes, glancing up at the mirror, from time to time locked on hers.

Who's this character? she wondered.

For the first part of the journey, she recognised the route from her own failed attempt to tail them in Alfie's truck, but then it seemed to take a different turning.

The sedan didn't actually race through the twisting streets, navigating the maze that was night-time Soho, but she could feel the rumble of a powerful engine. If the driver needed speed, it would be there.

She had to resist the temptation to turn and look out the rear window. She hoped that if she did she'd see a small pair of lights somewhere behind them.

Harry, in the Alvis, following.

But turning would only alert the driver. So, she sat there, facing forward, no one saying anything. The air heavy with an expectation of what was to come, so late in the night, morning only hours away.

Though Kat had walked into quite a few risky situations, at an embassy dinner, or a late meeting with a courier in some backwater café abroad, this was new.

And she was frightened.

"DAMN," Harry said, as the big saloon seemed to disappear into one curved street and then, so quickly into another.

"I'm going to lose him, Alfie."

"No. Okay. Take the next left. See it? Tenison Court. The way that bloke's headed, we'll catch him on the other side, on Regent Street."

Harry turned to him even as they got the Alvis squeezed between the buildings, down an alleyway that seemed more suited for livestock than a car. "No other turns it could take?"

But Alfie shook his head. "Car that big, you don't get a lot of options."

Alfie grinned in the darkness.

Always so pleased when he could be of help.

Damn good man, Harry thought.

The Alvis bumped down the alley, once even scraping a metal rubbish bin, until finally it emerged onto Regent Street.

"Can't see it! I don't—"

But Alfie pointed at the red lights speeding up the empty avenue, then slowing and taking a left.

"There he is. Heading towards Mayfair, as expected," Alfie said. "Should be smooth sailing from here."

"Great," Harry said, picking up speed, following. "Remind me never to visit Soho again in anything resembling this vehicle."

"Least not while you're driving, eh, boss?"

And with that break in the tension, they both laughed.

KAT PEERED out of the sedan's window as the driver pulled up beside a stately house. She could see curved wrought-iron grilles on all the windows, and an impressive stone staircase leading to a solid back door that – with its satiny sheen – picked up the glow from a nearby street lamp.

But that glow was now beginning to fade.

Like they were in a cloud.

And Kat remembered.

Right, London, gets fog. Evening cools down. The Thames nearby.

As the sedan stopped, the streetlight began to look like an impressionistic depiction of a massive candle, the fog now seeming to threaten the light completely.

The driver popped out.

"Right then, ladies, come on, come on. Night's not getting any younger."

Kat followed the others out, with Lizzie just in front.

She risked a whisper. "You know where we're going?"

The girl turned to her. No words. Just a nod.

LONDON CALLING!

Terribly sad.

They trooped up behind the driver as he knocked on the door. A variation of the Red Rabbit code – two sharp knocks. A pause. Then two more.

The door to the grand house opened.

Cigar and cigarette smoke billowed out to join the fog, which also gathered at the door.

And with the driver – their guide – keeping watch though the visibility was fading, Kat followed the other girls in.

HARRY stopped the Alvis.

"Bit close here," Alfie said, "Could be spotted."

"Chance we have to take. With this damn fog rolling in, not sure what we'll see."

And after watching the dancers disappear – *so strange to think that Kat was among them* – he waited.

The fog grew more dense.

"What a night," said Alfie. "Proper pea-souper."

Harry could only nod in reply. All this was starting to feel too dangerous. He saw some men arrive, their top hats visible, but in this mess of a fog, there was no way to see faces.

Could be anyone, Harry thought.

More men arrived, distinguishable only by their shape and size: this one tall; another shaped like a summer marrow; one having a spot of alcohol-fuelled trouble navigating the stone steps.

And then nothing.

Harry could wait no longer.

"I'm going to take a look."

"What? Boss, best not. I'll go there, take a—"

But Harry had already popped open the door of the Alvis, and started hurrying to the house, now himself just a shadowy figure on the fog-ridden street.

WHILE DRINKS got poured and passed around, Kat found herself suddenly cornered by a small man in a tux with a snow-white, perfectly trimmed moustache, his balding head covered by a few strands of hair, as if it could mask the shiny dome.

"So, is it true?" the man said, his eyes bright, eager.

Kat of course keeping a smile on her face.

But also thinking – *if this guy so much as lays a hand on me, well.*

She knew what to do in such cases. Quickly and effectively.

"What do you mean?" she said.

"You Americans." The man flashed a smile, his uneven teeth catching the light. About the toothiest smile she had seen in quite a while. "Always, brave, bold…" and here the man pumped his arm as if rallying the troops to pick up the pace, "adventurous?"

"Oh. Dunno about all that," Kat said. "I'm more the shy, retiring type." The man's face fell, either not getting the humour of the situation, or genuinely disappointed.

"Oh, um, well I—" the tubby tuxedoed man fumbled.

Kat guessed the men didn't have to try too hard with witty banter at this private party.

And as she looked around, she saw the girls all chatting, and one of them – Sally – sitting on one well-dressed man's lap, laughing up a storm.

Must be gold in them thar hills, Kat thought. *Exactly how "private" does this party get?*

But then, she saw Lizzie.

She had been cornered by a man who towered over her. And after looking left and right, as if seeking escape, she watched as Lizzie said something to the man, and then literally bolted away.

In the direction of the hallway to the bathroom, guessed Kat.

Presumably the one safe place in this joint.

And Kat knew what she had to do.

WITH A QUICK look up and down the street, Harry made his way up the steps to the big house, holding the hand rail. Part of him wanted to rap on that ominous-looking black door, and just get Kat.

But he reminded himself: *Steady. She can take care of herself.*

At the door, he leaned forward, hoping his hunch would pay off.

To see a name on the side by a brass doorbell.

Cedric Grosvenor.

And suddenly some things started to make sense.

But then he heard, on the other side of the door, steps.

Someone coming.

As the door handle turned, Harry raced down the steps, and – with the Alvis too far away to provide cover – he hopped over the metal gate that led to a downstairs flat, maybe to the servants' quarters.

He pressed against the wall by the stone stairs, in the darkness and the swirling fog, as just above his head, he heard a man walk out of the house and onto the steps.

From down here, no way to see the man's face. Just his shiny shoes, evening coat, a white scarf – and in one hand a large, brown envelope. Now, a movement as he popped a well-creased hat on his head.

Something familiar about that head.

The man reached the bottom of the steps, slipped the envelope into his coat pocket and then paused, as if he might be considering.

Home? Or a really late nightcap?

And as the man turned, Harry, invisible in the shadows, could finally see his profile, and he peered up through the black railings, to see…

Oliver Pleasance, the slimy new "friend" that he'd made back at the Town Hall in Mydworth.

The man obviously closely connected to Grosvenor's little operation here.

Which, Harry was beginning to think, was maybe not so little.

He watched, still crouching against the cold, damp stone as Pleasance turned and started walking away from the house.

And when he was safely steps away, Harry scurried back to the Alvis, staying low, though in truth the fog was proving useful as cover.

Inside the car he wasted no time.

"Alfie, see that chap? Got a favour to ask you."

To which Alfie answered by popping open his door. "Now don't you worry, Harry. Fog like this… perfect for following a bloke."

"Good man. Just need to know where he lives, maybe what he does with an envelope he just tucked into that coat."

"I'll do a proper recce." Alfie slipped out of the car. "You stay here for your Kat. Tomorrow, first thing, I'll let you know what I've found."

And with that, Alfie was gone, and Harry was left alone, looking at the building. Lights on, as if whoever lived there didn't know or didn't care that it was still the dead of night.

This party clearly not coming to an end any time soon.

LONDON CALLING!

13.

THE SORDID TRUTH

Kat hurried down the long, carpeted corridor, looking for the bathroom. She passed dull landscape paintings and faded portraits – the place looking to her more like a private club than a home.

Doors on either side – were they perhaps to offices, living rooms, or maybe bedrooms? One door was different from the others – and from inside, she heard the sound of muted crying.

The bathroom? Had to be. She tried the door – locked.

So, she leaned close. Tapped gently.

"Lizzie? Lizzie?"

Silence. Then a sniff, and a low voice from inside: "Yes? What?"

"Lizzie – can you let me in? Just for a second."

She waited.

"Please," Kat said, keeping her voice to a whisper.

A click. The door unlocked, and with a quick turn of the doorknob, Kat let herself in.

Lizzie, her mascara running, a crumpled tissue in her hands; the girl seeking refuge, some escape from the predatory men outside.

"Y-you okay?"

Lizzie gave Kat a rueful smile.

"Yeah, just *fine*."

Kat knew they wouldn't have much time. Whatever was going on outside, they'd be soon missed.

Chased down.

"Lizzie," she said, shutting the door behind her and locking it again. "Why are you doing this? Why not just leave?"

In the intimacy of the large bathroom, with its shiny golden taps, marble sinks and counter, Lizzie answered.

"Leave? Think it's that easy? Maybe for *you*. He's got nothing on you."

"He?"

"Grosvenor."

"The agent?" said Kat, not understanding. "*That* Grosvenor?"

"This is his house. Didn't you know?"

Kat shook her head. So Grosvenor was behind all this. The club. The parties.

"What's he got on you?" she said, already guessing the answer. Kat took a breath. "Photos?" said Kat. "That it?"

Lizzie said nothing, looked away. Then looked back at Kat, eyes red, and nodded.

"Not that I've done anything, you know... bad," said the girl. "Just... dressing up and stuff."

"Nobody's hurt you?" said Kat.

"No," said Lizzie. "Not yet."

"And these photos – he said he'd make them public?"

The girl nodded again. "But if I – what is it you Americans say? – 'play ball' all will be fine."

Extortion, thought Kat. And it wasn't her first experience of it. On foreign postings, when State Department officials had found themselves in potentially embarrassing situations, Kat had often been tasked to dig them out of their holes.

Now she had a hunch.

Maybe Lizzie wasn't the only one here, trapped in this life.

"Look – I think I can help."

"You – you're not really a dancer, are you?"

Kat smiled, and put a hand on the girl's shoulder.

"No, I'm not. But listen – I don't think I can just take you out of here now. Tonight. They might make good on their threat. Lizzie, do you think you can stick with this, just one more day? Then – my word – it will end."

"Your word? Whatever can you—?"

A knock at the door.

"Come *on*! People out here. They're wanting a show. Get a move on!"

Kat gave her shoulder a squeeze. "Trust me. I can help. Okay?"

The girl hesitated.

Kat wondered if it had been a long time since Lizzie had trusted anyone. Then, as if it was a giant leap of faith, considering the world she was trapped in and the people she was dealing with, Lizzie Spence said, "I will."

"Good girl," Kat said. "Just get through tonight."

She unlocked the door and poked her head out to look down the corridor.

Empty. Whoever had been sent to retrieve them, had gone. She opened the door wider, and stepped back to let Lizzie out.

Then she watched as the young girl headed back towards the party. If that was the right word for it.

Kat could hear a new song distantly playing on the Victrola.

One that seemed about as inappropriate as could be.

Eddie Cantor, crooning about "Making Whoopee".

Somehow she was going to have to get out of here. Not the way she'd come in – that was for sure. But she had a good idea how to do it.

Back in New York, when she was scrambling to earn money to get through college, she'd worked as a maid in big houses like this.

And she knew how they functioned – how below-stairs rooms and corridors fitted snug like shadows to the public areas. With their own ways in and out.

Checking the corridor was still empty, she turned the other way, walking fast, looking for a service door. Such doors unmarked, usually without a handle.

Right at the end – and there it was. She pushed against it, swung it open to reveal a narrow flight of stairs.

Bingo!

She stepped through and shut the door carefully – but then a sound in the corridor behind her made her pause. A conversation. Low voices – people approaching, then stopping, the discussion continuing.

She gently pushed the door open again just half an inch, peered through the gap.

Across the corridor, she could see one of the other doors was now open, revealing what looked like an office. Inside – a desk, chairs, shelves loaded with files.

In the doorway, with his back to her – she saw Charlie Leet, the club bouncer.

Looking about as out of place as he could be.

And beyond him, another man she didn't recognise from the "party" room: glossy, corpulent, in a slick dress suit, monocle in one eye.

The man was stooped over a large safe.

A classic safe that she recognised. An American Mosler.

"What about booze?" said the man over his shoulder. "Bar stocked?"

"Plenty, Mr Grosvenor. Got a few pills too, if anyone asks."

So this is Grosvenor, thought Kat, not surprised. If ever a man looked like his voice sounded, here he was.

"Excellent," said Grosvenor. She watched him, as he unfolded a small piece of paper and started to read from it – while he turned the tumblers of the safe.

Kat held her breath, peering through the tiniest gap in the open door, watching.

Grosvenor entered the final number, then reached across and pulled the heavy lever.

The safe opened.

And even from this distance, Kat could see inside. Stacks of banknotes. Folders. Envelopes.

Grosvenor turned back to Leet who handed him a wad of banknotes.

"They all paid up then?" said Grosvenor, taking the money.

"Every one," said Leet.

Kat watched Grosvenor lick one finger and quickly count the notes, before wrapping a band around them and placing them in the safe. Then she saw him reach in, remove a camera with a flash, and hand it to Leet.

Then he closed the safe, spun the combination wheel.

Kat kept her eyes on the piece of paper in Grosvenor's hand – but Leet stepped in the way at the last moment – and when he stood aside, the paper with the combination was no longer visible.

Damn, she thought. *Now that could have been useful.*

Had he slipped it in his pocket? Put it in one of the files on the shelves? In the desk?

She didn't know.

She watched, as both men now turned and came back to the door, then stepped out into the corridor. Neither of them noticing the service door, just slightly open, where Kat still peered through.

She saw Grosvenor take a key from his pocket and lock the door. Then the two men headed back in the direction of the party, with Leet carrying the camera.

When they'd gone, she quickly slipped back into the corridor, tried the door – just in case – but no, definitely locked.

There was no way she could get in there tonight. But at least now she had a good idea where Grosvenor kept the incriminating photographs of the girls.

She headed back through the service door, and tiptoed down two flights of steps, until she emerged in what looked like a storeroom, shelves loaded with wooden crates of soda, bottles of beer, wine.

Not a sound in this part of the house. The servants probably given the weekend evenings off, when there was "entertainment" planned above stairs.

She walked through the storeroom, the only light coming through high windows that looked up through gratings onto the street lamps outside.

At the back of the storeroom, a door. Next to it a rack of keys, each one carefully labelled.

She looked at them in the dim light, and made out two keys marked "kitchen door".

Taking care to make no sound, she tried them in the door. They both worked, the door popping open. She put one back on the rack, opened the door – and stepped out into a small, below street level courtyard.

She locked the door again, slipped the key into her pocket.

Turning, she now saw a worn flight of stone steps that led up to a gate. Crouching, she climbed the steps, opened the gate and slipped through, shutting it silently behind her.

She was out!

LONDON CALLING!

She breathed a sigh of relief. She was back in the street, in the fog and the yellow light from the lamps.

Safe.

She looked down the street, along the side of the great house from which she'd just emerged. And she could just see the familiar shape of the Alvis. With the key clutched in one hand, she walked towards the car, her sparkling heels clicking on the sidewalk.

Thinking – *God – what must I look like?*

No coat, in her sparkling tights, sequinned top and tiny bits of red fur…

She walked up to the car, then leaned down by the passenger window and peered in.

Harry's smiling face looked back at her.

She watched him lean across and open the door.

"Well, hello," he said. "Out for a stroll? Spot of fresh air?"

She shook her head, grinning as she climbed into the car, and sank back, relieved, into the leather seat.

"Kat – you okay?" he said, placing his hand on hers.

Kat nodded. "I am. The other girls up there though… Where's Alfie?"

"On a tail," he said. "We staying here?"

"No, we can head back," said Kat. Another smile. "Done for the night."

"But – let me guess. Got a plan?"

"Kinda," she said.

"That's good," he said, starting the engine and pulling quietly away. "I do like plans. So very useful."

As they drove down the empty street towards Bloomsbury, Kat could see the first hint of dawn in the sky ahead, over the tall London houses.

It had been such a long night.

And she felt, now, it was going to be a long day too.

LONDON CALLING!

14.

BREAKFAST MEETING

Harry woke to the sound of the telephone ringing all too loudly in the other room, and was instantly alert.

He looked across at Kat – who still slept soundly – then slipped quietly out of bed, put on his dressing gown, and went through to take the call, gently closing the door behind him.

They'd only had a couple of hours' sleep, after sitting together over tea and toast, quickly catching up with the night's events.

He picked up the receiver.

"Museum 642," he said, then waited for the pips to finish. The call was from a telephone box.

"Harry," came Alfie's voice.

"Alfie. What news?"

"Followed Pleasance to a block in Pimlico, where he stayed all night," said Alfie. "Six-thirty sharp, he comes out, takes a bus to Bank. I hopped on, without him seeing."

"Good man! And?"

"Right now, he's in the tea rooms on Ludgate Hill. Reckon he's meeting someone. Thought you should know."

"You got eyes on him now, Alfie?"

"Call box opposite, boss. He's got a seat, right by the window."

"I'm on my way. If he moves, stay with him. We can both phone in here, Kat can liaise."

"Gotcha."

"One more thing. He still got that envelope?"

"Like it's glued to him."

"Be with you in twenty minutes, Alfie."

Harry put down the phone, then went back to the bedroom to wake Kat – and tell her the latest addition to their plan.

"Wakey, wakey," he said, leaning down to her.

KAT SAT alongside Harry in the back of the cab, glad of her coat on this chilly morning. They wove through a maze of busy streets on their way to Ludgate Hill, the city alive with a throng of determined workers heading to offices, markets and stores.

There was no way she was going to stay back in the apartment and let Harry have all the fun. So the two of them had dressed fast, and gotten out of the door and picked up a cab in a fast five minutes.

"Oh, this is Fleet Street," said Harry, as they paid the cab and emerged onto a highway busy with buses, taxis and trams – as well as some horses and carts. "Very famous, and all that."

On either side of the bustling street she could see newspaper offices and giant billboards. On the corners, boys shouting, selling their stacks of the day's news. And just visible between the buildings, the distant dome of St Paul's.

It was quite something.

Just a minute later they reached Ludgate Hill, and she saw Alfie standing by a call box, looking like he was reading the morning paper but with his eyes locked on the tea rooms on the other side of the street.

LONDON CALLING!

"He still there?" said Harry, shaking Alfie's hand as they both slipped into the cover provided by the call box.

"Window in the corner," said Alfie, nodding to the tea rooms.

Kat looked across and, through the gaps in the rush-hour traffic, saw a face she recognised from the club, sitting alone at a table in the bustling room, a mug of tea in front of him.

"That's Pleasance all right," said Harry. "And well... what do you know? Kat, look!"

He gestured to a man in a raincoat, crossing the street, head down, heading towards the tea rooms.

At the door, the man turned and gave a nervous glance over his shoulder – and Kat recognised him instantly.

"Aubrey Spence!" she said, as he slipped into the tea rooms. "What's he doing here? Can't be a coincidence."

"Indeed not," said Harry as she saw Spence pull up the chair opposite Pleasance.

"That Lizzie's old man?" said Alfie. Kat nodded. "*Strewth.* He involved in this racket too?"

"Right now, I have no idea," said Kat. "But, if he is, it would certainly explain why he didn't want us on the case."

As they watched, Pleasance took out the envelope from his jacket pocket and slid it across the table to Lizzie's father – who then took out a smaller envelope from his own pocket and handed it to Pleasance.

Pleasance nodded, looked around, then got up from the table, crossed the room and appeared at the door onto the street.

"You want me to stay on his tail?" said Alfie.

"No need," said Harry. "Get some sleep, old friend – and we'll give you a ring this afternoon. Methinks today is going to get rather hectic."

Kat saw Alfie nod, then fold his newspaper and slip away into the crowd. A few seconds later, it was as if he'd never been there.

"Time to have another chat with Aubrey, don't you think?" said Kat.

"Absolutely," said Harry. "Mug of tea and a bacon sandwich too while we're at it."

"Heaven," said Kat. And together they crossed Ludgate Hill, dodging buses and trucks, and entered the tea rooms.

"WHAT THE HELL are you two doing here?" said Aubrey Spence, looking up from his tea as Harry sat opposite him. Harry saw that Spence was shocked. And maybe a bit afraid.

"I might well ask you the same thing," said Kat, taking the seat next to Aubrey and clearly shocking him even more.

Harry saw the man's eyes dart from one to the other behind the small round spectacles, a glossy sheen of sweat appearing on his pink, domed forehead.

"Th-this is preposterous!" said Aubrey, pushing his chair back and beginning to stand – until Kat's firm hand on his shoulder made him pause.

Harry saw Kat, in one deft move, slip her other hand into Aubrey's jacket pocket, remove the envelope and slide it across the table to him.

"Dammit, you can't just—" said Aubrey, leaning forward and trying to snatch the envelope back. "This isn't America! The Wild West! You can't—"

But Harry held the envelope close – just as the woman from behind the counter forced Aubrey to sit back by sliding mugs and plates onto the table.

"Two teas, two bacon sandwiches, one special with a lovely fried egg!" she said, and was gone as quickly as she'd arrived.

Harry smiled at Aubrey, passed the plate and mug to Kat, and took a sip of tea.

"Needed that," he said, watching Kat dig into her bacon sandwich.

"Ooh, me too," said Kat, mouth full. "When *was* the last time we ate?"

"What the *hell's* going on?" said Aubrey. "I'm going to call the police!"

"Oh, I wouldn't do that, Aubrey, old pal," said Harry. "Not unless you want to explain why you're buying photos of dancing girls – and I'm guessing here – in all sorts of *indelicate* states of undress? Respectable gentleman like yourself?"

He opened the envelope and peeked inside, shook his head, then peered at Aubrey as he tried to calculate what was happening, his eyes blinking behind those round glasses.

Aubrey seemed shaken, as though his bluster was about to be replaced with something else – something much more dire.

"I'm not *buying* the photographs," he said. "It isn't like that at all, not at all."

"Isn't it?" said Kat. "It's what it looks like to us."

"Oh God," said Aubrey, shaking his head. "This is the end. I'm ruined. Ruined."

"Quite possibly," said Kat. "And from where I'm sitting, maybe you deserve to be."

"I told you two not to get involved, didn't I?" said Aubrey.

"And it's a very good thing we ignored your request," said Harry. "At least with us around Lizzie has a chance to get out of whatever mess she's in."

Spence shook his head.

"You can't help her. Nobody can."

Harry saw Aubrey put his head into his hands then stare back at them both, his eyes red.

"You got an explanation, Mr Spence?" said Kat. "Because if you do, we need to hear it."

Harry took another sip of tea, waited as Aubrey appeared to weigh up all the options.

"All right," he said, looking around the busy tea room and leaning forward, speaking softly. "I'll tell you."

"WHEN LIZZIE first disappeared, we waited, of course, a few days for her to get in contact," said Aubrey. "But then there was no news. Nothing at all. So I started to stay late in town after work – go round the theatres, see if anyone had seen her. Perhaps knew where she might be. But nobody had!"

The plates had been cleared away, and Kat had moved round the table to sit next to Harry – so she could see Aubrey's face clearly.

Look for any lies.

So far, he seemed to be telling the truth. In fact, she could see him struggling not to break down completely.

"It was as if she'd just disappeared into thin air," he continued. "Then, one day, in the office, I got a letter in the post. It contained… a photograph."

"Of Lizzie, yes?" said Harry. "A photograph like one of these?"

"Yes, yes – and it was awful," said Aubrey, nodding. "Devastating. I couldn't believe…"

"Go on," said Kat, as Aubrey wiped his eyes with his handkerchief.

"There was a letter with it. It said I had to come here, the next morning, sit in this corner, and somebody would come and talk to me, about Lizzie. I didn't know what to expect. I thought perhaps someone had rescued her, was going to help us."

"But they didn't want to help, did they?" said Kat. "They wanted to blackmail you."

She saw Aubrey nod.

"The man who came, who was here just now, you know him, don't you?" said Aubrey. "I saw you talking to him in Mydworth."

"Oliver Pleasance," said Harry.

"Pleasance," Spence shook his head. "Scum of the earth. He said, *oh yes*, Lizzie was safe. But she'd fallen in with a bad crowd. Said there were more photographs. Lots of them. But he could get them, stop them being made public. Make sure nobody at my company, Imperial, saw them… and nobody back at Mydworth."

"As long as you paid up," said Harry.

"For the effort of getting hold of them, he said. So… I did."

"How much?" said Kat.

"Fifty pounds," said Aubrey.

"Phew," said Kat. *A small fortune.*

"Then – let me guess," said Harry, "a week later, you got another letter, asking for more."

"You're right – but how did you know?"

"It's a very old game," said Kat. "A mug's game. Get the fish on the hook and keep it wriggling there."

"And I'm the fish, I suppose?" said Aubrey, his shoulders slumped.

"How many times?" said Harry.

"Today's the fourth. Each time I give him the money, he says it's over and that Lizzie will come home. But it never is. And she never comes home."

"Two hundred pounds?" said Kat. "My God, you could buy a car with that!"

Kat saw Harry look at her, figuring something else out.

She listened carefully, Harry's voice low.

"Where did you get the money, Aubrey?" said Harry.

Kat saw Aubrey blink again – his automatic response to any difficult question.

"I... I... There's one of the investment accounts I administer for Imperial. I have sole authority, I can make withdrawals you see, so I..."

"You stole it," said Harry, his voice still low.

"Yes," said Aubrey.

"And nobody at the office has found out?"

"Not yet. But there's an audit next week. The missing money will certainly be spotted. And that will be the end of it. Of me. Of Lizzie. Of everything."

As Aubrey put his head in his hands again, Kat knew now that he was telling the truth. He simply didn't have the cunning to lie. He seemed totally broken.

Then she looked at Harry, an idea beginning to form.

The beginnings of a plan.

"Aubrey, tell me. Do you have a way of contacting Pleasance?"

"There's an emergency phone number if I can't meet him. It's just some kind of answering service, I think."

"Good," she said. "And this evening – if you have to – can you stay in town?"

"I suppose so. Yes. Why? Do you think you can help me?"

Kat looked at Harry. She reached across the table, put her hand on Aubrey's sleeve.

"I don't know – yet. I can't promise anything. Sir Harry and I will have to talk. But first you need to go *back* to the office. Then, when we know what we're going to do, we'll telephone you. Okay?"

Kat saw a flicker of hope in Aubrey's eyes. She didn't want to raise that hope too high, but the more she thought things through, the more she thought she could see a way out of this abyss.

A way to free Lizzie, destroy Grosvenor.

Maybe even get Aubrey's money back – and save his career.

15.

IT'S ALL IN THE TIMING

Harry sat with Aubrey Spence in the American Bar of the Savoy Hotel, sipping his gin and tonic and keeping an eye on the entrance, reflected in the glitzy Art Deco mirror behind the bar.

He checked his watch − six-thirty.

Half an hour to go, a table for three in the Savoy Grill Room already booked. (After having to pull a few strings at such short notice, *"For you, Sir Harry, of course."*)

He and Aubrey had arrived early, in case Grosvenor should feel an urge to try some kind of recce.

That's what Harry would have done, had *he* been expecting to walk away from a meeting five hundred pounds richer − in cash.

In fact, he would have placed at least a couple of heavies in strategic positions, in case the meeting went to pot.

But so far, nothing to report.

The Head Waiter (who remembered him from years back) had completely understood when Harry requested that his name not be uttered by any of the staff.

This plan − this whole, wonderful, daring plan, as devised by Lady Mortimer herself − depended on Cedric Grosvenor *believing* that Harry was simply a work colleague of Aubrey's, here to give moral support and witness the transaction.

No suspicion of him actually being undercover.

Grosvenor had Spence so cowed, it was unlikely he'd suspect him of doing anything other than follow their rules.

Harry looked at the man who sat next to him nursing a scotch, eyes anxiously flitting at each new arrival.

"Chin up, Aubrey," said Harry. "Hearts of oak, stiff upper, you know the drill…"

Aubrey took a miniscule sip of his scotch and nodded nervously.

"I-I can't remember a word of what I'm supposed to say," he said.

"Oh, don't worry about that," said Harry cheerfully. "I'll say it if you don't. Improvisation, hmm?"

"And what if he wants to inspect the money?" said Aubrey, nodding to the briefcase at his feet. "I mean – *really* inspect it."

"Ah, yes. Well, we'll deal with that when it happens," said Harry. "*If* it happens."

Then he smiled at the barman. "Top-up please, Ralph, when you have a moment."

"Certainly, Mr… *Smith*," said Ralph. "Right away."

Harry smiled. The service at the Savoy – as ever – at its most impeccable.

And always discreet *for the right people*.

KAT SAT with Alfie in the front seat of his truck, watching the front door of the smart Grosvenor residence.

With no make-up, wearing overalls and one of Alfie's brown workmen's coats, and a flat cap pulled down to her eyebrows, Kat guessed that she made the perfect young apprentice.

She checked her watch. If Grosvenor had taken the bait – Aubrey's telephoned offer of one final big payment, paid in person to the owner of the photographs — surely he had to be leaving now to get to the Savoy in time for the handover?

But she didn't need to worry.

"There he is," said Alfie.

Kat watched as the imposing black door opened and Grosvenor emerged with Charlie Leet.

The two of them went down the steps to where the big sedan was parked. And, as Grosvenor climbed in the back, Leet got in the driving seat and started up the engine.

Kat waited until the sedan had pulled away and disappeared in the direction of the Strand. Then, with a quick nod to Alfie, she climbed out of the truck and went round to the back doors.

Alfie opened them, reached in and slid out a couple of cases of champagne. She took one of the cases, he took the other.

And they crossed the road to the servants' entrance of Grosvenor's house.

Down the stone steps to the door Kat had come through last night.

Alfie pulled on a small bell that hung by the door and they waited. No answer.

She looked at Alfie. "Empty house — I hope."

Then she put down her case, took out the key that she'd stolen, slipped it in the lock, and opened the door.

INSIDE — darkness, and silence. If she was right, the day staff had gone home, and whatever evening staff Grosvenor used for his soirees hadn't arrived yet.

If I'm right, she thought. *And if not…*

"Alfie — if I'm not out in half an hour," she said, picking up her case of wine and adding it to his, "you'll—"

"Come right up for *yer*? No fear about that. And good luck," said Alfie, tipping his cap to her and heading back up the stairs with his heavy load.

Kat watched him disappear, then she shut the door, and headed deeper into the house.

HARRY LEANED back against the velvet of the banquette, took a sip of what – not surprisingly – was a truly excellent Pomerol, and surveyed the famed Savoy Grill Room.

Although still early, the place was filling up. From here – his chosen table in the corner – he had the perfect field of vision.

He smiled encouragingly at Aubrey, who sat opposite, fiddling with his napkin.

"Not long now, Aubrey," he said. "Just stay steady."

Aubrey blinked, wiped his sweaty brow with his handkerchief.

Then Harry saw Grosvenor, arriving at the entrance area. Kat's description of the man was detailed – it had to be him.

He watched as the maître d' led Grosvenor over to Harry's table.

Harry quickly built a first impression: Grosvenor was overweight and portly, but his dress suit looked expensive, and perfectly tailored for his girth. He'd arrived alone – so his man was probably outside in the car.

And Harry noticed no *goons* taking places at the Grill's doors.

Grosvenor was all alone.

He carried no attaché case – so whatever deal he'd been expecting to make this evening with Spence, it clearly didn't involve handing over any photographs.

For a second, as Grosvenor approached the table, Harry could see a flicker of surprise on the man's face as he realised there were three of them dining together, not two – but that surprise was slickly concealed.

"Mr Spence?" said Grosvenor, holding out his hand, as Aubrey and Harry stood to greet him.

"I'm Spence," said Aubrey, not taking the proffered handshake.

"Smith," said Harry genially, gripping Grosvenor's hand firmly.

"Smith?" said Grosvenor, his lip curling with a smile, as the three of them sat down at the table. "I wasn't expecting to dine *à trois*."

"Here to give my friend Aubrey some, well, moral support," said Harry.

"Of course. Very good. Mr *Smith*."

Harry noted that Grosvenor hadn't revealed his name – and clearly didn't intend to.

"Excellent choice of venue," said Grosvenor. "Very civilised."

"No reason why this little, arrangement, cannot be conducted in a gentlemanly fashion," said Harry. "That's what Aubrey here said, right?"

Harry looked at the wobbly Spence who – all nerves now – could only manage a quick nod.

"Exactly," said Grosvenor, unravelling his napkin from its silver holder and placing it on his lap. "My attitude entirely."

Then Harry saw him look to Aubrey then back again.

"But before we commence – what I am sure shall be a most *delightful* repast – may I just ask you to confirm that you do indeed have the wherewithal to complete our little transaction?"

Harry saw Aubrey look alarmed – and nodded to the briefcase that stood under the table by Aubrey's feet.

He watched as Aubrey lifted it up, opened it nervously, for Grosvenor to peer in.

Harry knew the contents: rolls of paper carefully wrapped in five-pound notes.

Same old trick, he thought. *Always works.*

"Jolly good," said Grosvenor, leaning back in his seat, and taking the menu from the waiter who had just appeared at his side. "How's the lobster tonight?"

KAT PRESSED her ear against the cold steel of the Mosler safe, and gently rotated the dial, listening for the tumblers to click.

Getting up the stairs and into the office had been a piece of cake. No sign of anyone in the house – though she'd been careful not to make a sound.

The only fly in the ointment had been the absence of the scrap of paper with the combination on it. Grosvenor clearly kept it tight.

But so far, the classic safe was behaving itself.

Years ago, when she'd first signed up to government service, she'd been taught to work safes just like this one. In fact, her first success in the field had been a Mosler, deep within the Turkish embassy.

Kinda like these old brutes, she thought, as the final number clicked into place and she heard the tumblers fall.

"Gotcha," she whispered to herself, this whole escapade going sweetly to plan.

Then she reached across for the lever and with both hands turned it. Slowly the heavy door pulled open and she could see inside.

The safe was *crammed*. On one shelf – stacks of banknotes. Hundreds – maybe even thousands of pounds.

And on a shelf below – photographs. Plenty of them. She picked them up and leafed through them. Compromising pictures – of all kinds, featuring the dancers – and a variety of different men.

Some of whom, she recognised. Famous people from public life, from both sides of the Atlantic.

And certainly not the kind of snaps you'd take on holiday – or show your mom, she thought.

Or your wife.

She took out a folded canvas bag from the deep pocket of her workman's coat, and started to fill it with the money and the photos.

Which was when she heard a sound from right behind her.

"Well, well, well," came a man's voice. "If it ain't the *Yankee* dancer from the club."

Kat turned to see Oliver Pleasance, standing in the doorway.

"Now – you'd better put those things back in the safe, pretty lady," said Pleasance. "Or Oliver here is going to have to teach you a little lesson. Naughty, naughty."

Kat stood up, put the bag on the floor and smiled sweetly.

"A lesson? From you, Mr Pleasance?" she said. "Oh, I can't wait."

And as Pleasance grinned and lurched forward, Kat was already figuring out what punishment she was going to give him for his part in this nasty little operation.

LONDON CALLING!

16.

GAME OVER

Harry watched Cedric Grosvenor take a final mouthful of crème brûlée, then push the plate to one side, tip the last of the 1920 Chateau d'Yquem into his glass and swallow it.

"Very decent," said Grosvenor, wiping his ample lips with his napkin. "Very decent *indeed*."

Harry smiled and nodded. He glanced down at his watch.

Eight thirty, he thought. *Kat should have been here by now. Unless something has gone wrong...*

"And so – to business, yes?" said Grosvenor.

Harry nodded. Nudged Aubrey, who nodded too. Grosvenor sat back, hands clasped on his bulging stomach.

"If I recall rightly from the message relayed to me earlier today, you – Mr Spence – have proposed one final payment to me of five hundred pounds cash, in return for which I hand over to you all evidence of your daughter's unfortunate... *fall from grace*, which – I can assure you – is currently in my possession. Correct?"

Spence cleared his throat. "Correct."

"As the man says... *correct*," said Harry, smiling, all *bonhomie*, even as his eyes flicked to the Grill Room entrance, but catching no sign of Kat.

"An interesting proposal," said Grosvenor. "But sadly, I'm afraid one that woefully underestimates the value of those *items*."

"What?" said Aubrey, sounding genuinely alarmed.

"You see – such photographs command a premium fee on the open market, Mr Spence. You must understand, your daughter is not only a very talented and attractive young woman, but with such an important, respected father? Well, I am sure you understand. These pictures… so very valuable." He cleared his throat and leaned close. "And – in the wrong hands – so very dangerous."

"Gosh. So are you saying that you would like *more* money?" said Harry bluntly. "That it?"

"Like? No. *Require.*"

"And what about the photographs? I assume you haven't brought them?"

"In here?" said Grosvenor as if the notion were outlandish. "To the Savoy Grill Room? Of course not. They're with my driver, outside."

"Really, Mr Grosvenor?" came Kat's voice from the side of the table.

Harry looked round – surprised – to see Kat, in long black evening gown, hair perfect, pearl earrings, diamond necklace and sparkling smile to match.

Looking a million bucks, thought Harry, using her own expression.

He watched as Kat drifted around the table slowly, walking past Aubrey and then Grosvenor, to stand by Harry's side. He felt her hand on his shoulder.

"I find what you just said there about the photographs very hard to believe," continued Kat.

"I beg your pardon, *madam* – I don't believe we've had the pleasure," said Grosvenor, standing up and looking confused at the sudden development.

LONDON CALLING!

"To recapitulate, Grosvenor, you were *saying*," said Harry, "that the photographs are with your driver?"

"That's right," he said nervously, clearly aware that the game had shifted. Then to Kat: "But, madam – you appear to be suggesting they are not?"

"Oh, I'm only going by what the helpful Mr Pleasance told me, earlier this evening," said Kat.

"What?"

"Apparently you laughed at the notion you would ever part with the photos. And suggested there were plenty more to be had where they came from."

"I don't know what you're talking about!" said Grosvenor. "Where did you meet Pleasance? Where is he?"

"Oh, he's rather 'tied up' right now I'm afraid," said Kat. "And – poor thing – he's suffering from an awfully bruised jaw. Bad fall, you know? Or something."

Grosvenor hurled his napkin onto the table.

"What the *hell* is going on here?" he said, through gritted teeth. "I demand to know!"

Harry saw nearby tables looking over.

Kat reached down to a bag by her feet, lifted a stack of folders and dropped them on the table.

"I'll tell you what's going on *Mister* Grosvenor," she said. "*You*, sir, are being turned over."

Harry saw Grosvenor step back in shock as he clearly recognised the folders from his safe.

"You can't... But these are from my private—"

"Very observant! They are indeed," said Harry, walking round the table to stand right in front of Grosvenor. "So, now, you listen to me. What you are doing – this racket – stops now. All of it. The club. You will close that, of course. The photographs. The parties. The girls. All gone. Or we take all of this to the police."

"And the only reason we're not getting the authorities involved now," said Kat, scooping up the folders, "is to protect the identity of those girls you've hurt – and continue to exploit."

Harry saw Grosvenor's eyes bulging, fit to burst, his face puce, his breathing fast.

Around them, the whole of the Savoy Grill had gone deathly quiet. Though few of the other diners would have heard the details of the conversation, it was clear that here... something momentous was going on.

Harry turned to Spence – looking ever more rattled – and nodded at him to get up. Then he called the waiter who hurried over.

"Delightful dinner, Charles – as ever," he said. "Mr Grosvenor's paying, of course. So kind."

He looked across at Kat – a triumphant warrior queen in his eyes.

"Shall we?" he said.

"Oh – one last thing," said Kat, stepping over to Grosvenor. "I have a message from some mutual friends, who I just collected from an address in Lexington Street and who are all delighted to know they'll never have to go to one of your parties again."

Uh-oh, thought Harry, seeing the way Kat had shifted her feet slightly. *I think I know what's coming...*

"Message?" said Grosvenor, looking confused. "What message?"

"This one."

To the amazement of the other hundred or so diners of the Savoy Grill Room, Kat Reilly – aka, Lady Mortimer of the Dower

House, Mydworth, Sussex – swung a perfect right hook full into Cedric Grosvenor's chin...

And Harry watched as the man dropped like a dead weight to the polished floor.

17.

ROYAL BOX

Kat leaned on the velvet edge of the best box in the Gaiety Theatre and watched as the audience hurried to their seats, just minutes now till curtain up.

So totally *thrilling* to be here now, her first London musical, Harry at her side, and her new and amazing friend Max Schultz being the most wonderful, generous, amazing host.

Generous – not just in providing this box and bottles of champagne – but in getting young Lizzie Spence an audition.

Which she *aced*, and then promptly got a part in the "London Follies" itself!

She turned. "A toast," she said, "to you, Max, and to my darling husband for being clever enough to make you his – and now my – good friend!"

"*Enchanté*," said Max clinking his glass with hers. "But really it is *you* we should toast, not just for gracing us with your presence here – but also for squashing that nasty, miserable cockroach Grosvenor. That – was something rather spectacular. You are my new hero, Kat Reilly!"

"Let's not forget, Harry played his part too," said Kat, clinking glasses with her husband.

"Harry? Oh, I'm *sure* he did," said Max.

LONDON CALLING!

"Too kind, Max, too kind," said Harry.

"But you, Lady Mortimer," continued Max, "you must know, you are the talk of London society."

"Well you know what they say about 'talk'."

Then Kat sat back in her plush seat, the orchestra below getting ready to play.

"Of course," said Max. "Nobody knows quite *why* you did what you did – just that Grosvenor was deeply dishonourable, and you were somehow righting a grievous wrong. At the Savoy Grill, no less!"

"A wrong righted? Long may it remain that way," said Kat. "It's just such a shame that Lizzie's parents couldn't be–"

"Hell-lo! Lizzie's parents?" came Nicola Green's voice from the open door of the box. "They're right here! Just made it."

Kat looked up to see Nicola standing with Aubrey and Glenys Spence, arm in arm, and all dressed up to the nines.

"Gosh!" said Glenys. "That train! So slow! I thought we'd *never* get here!"

Kat looked at Aubrey, who nodded and half-smiled at her and Harry.

They'd made an agreement – with Lizzie and Nicola too – that Glenys should never know what really happened in Lizzie's missing weeks in London.

And Glenys – it seemed – was so thrilled by Lizzie landing a part in this year's hit West End musical that she'd barely mentioned it.

Kat looked across at Nicola as the new arrivals all took their seats and the house lights went down.

As the overture began – a bouncy, innocent, carefree number – she felt Harry's hand on hers, giving it a gentle squeeze.

When the curtain went up – and the chorus line spun onto the stage, and Lizzie Spence high-kicked her way into her debut performance – Kat felt a thrill of relief and joy at what she and Harry had achieved…

… followed by just a *twinge* of pain in that hand to remind her to be more careful of how she formed a fist next time she had to lay somebody out.

Because – she knew for sure – there would be a next time.

London, Mydworth – wherever she and Harry ended up – it was always going to be eventful!

LONDON CALLING!

NEXT IN THE SERIES:

MURDER WORE A MASK

MYDWORTH MYSTERIES

Matthew Costello & Neil Richards

Lavinia's annual Masked Ball at Mydworth Manor is a highlight of the season, as locals mingle with the great and famous from London. But the lavish party comes to a full stop when one of the guests is found dead, down by the lake. It seems it's a clear case of a heart attack. But Harry and Kat suspect that the dead man in a mask was in fact the victim of a clever case of murder. And the killer's work at the party is not yet done...

ABOUT THE AUTHORS

Co-authors Neil Richards (based in the UK) and Matthew Costello (based in the US), have been writing together since the mid-90s, creating innovative television, games and best-selling books. Together, they have worked on major projects for the BBC, PBS, Disney Channel, Sony, ABC, Eidos, and Nintendo to name but a few.

Their transatlantic collaboration led to the globally best-selling mystery series, *Cherringham*, which has also been a top-seller as audiobooks read by Neil Dudgeon.

Mydworth Mysteries is their brand new series, set in 1929 Sussex, England, which takes readers back to a world where solving crimes was more difficult — but also sometimes a lot more fun.

LONDON CALLING!

Printed in the USA
CPSIA information can be obtained
at www.ICGtesting.com
LVHW051315070923
757244LV00009B/718